GRADUATION SUMMER

Never Say Good-bye

By Nancy Butcher

▰ HarperEntertainment
An Imprint of HarperCollins*Publishers*

A PARACHUTE PRESS BOOK

A PARACHUTE PRESS BOOK

Parachute Publishing, L.L.C.
156 Fifth Avenue, Suite 302
New York, NY 10010

Published by
HarperEntertainment
An Imprint of HarperCollins*Publishers*
10 East 53rd Street, New York, NY 10022-5299

GRADUATION SUMMER books are created and produced by Parachute Publishing, L.L.C., in cooperation with Dualstar Publications, a division of Dualstar Entertainment Group, LLC., published by HarperEntertainment, an imprint of HarperCollins Publishers.

ISBN 0-06-072283-5

First printing: August 2004

Printed in the United States of America

Visit HarperEntertainment on the World Wide Web at
www.harpercollins.com

10 9 8 7 6 5 4 3 2 1

CHAPTER ONE

Your Honor, I object!" Ashley Olsen called out.

She tossed her dark blond hair over her shoulders and narrowed her eyes at the mirror. She really *looked* like a lawyer—especially in her brand-new gray pin-striped jacket and matching skirt. A pearl necklace would help, though. She made a mental note to raid her mother's jewelry box ASAP.

"Overruled," her sister, Mary-Kate, piped up from her place on Ashley's bed. "You're not a lawyer—yet."

"I'm going to be working at Atwater, Bumble, and Chang all summer. That's close enough," Ashley pointed out. "Humor me, okay? I've got to get the hang of this."

She struck a pose, trying to look like one of the lawyers on television. "Your Honor, I'd like to call the next witness to the stand!"

The bedroom door opened, and the sisters' best friends, Felicity Lopez and Claudia Pierce, came in. They were both dressed in bikinis, sarongs, and flip-flops.

"A witness for what?" Felicity asked.

"Ashley is, um, trying her first case," Mary-Kate explained.

"'The Case of the Matching Bikinis!'" Claudia giggled, twirling around. "Felicity and I each got this same bikini in five different colors. I got it in magenta, spruce, lime, black, and silver—"

"—and I got it in bronze, royal blue, white, yellow, and fuchsia," Felicity finished. "A girl can't be wearing the same color bikini to work every day!"

Ashley relaxed her lawyer pose and checked out her friends' outfits. Felicity and Claudia looked more stylish than ready for their summer jobs at the beach club. And Mary-Kate looked very *Seabiscuit* in her new riding clothes. She had a summer job at the Silver Spurs Stables, where she would lead tourists on trail rides, clean out stalls, and do other horsey things Ashley had no interest in.

Ashley and the other girls had just passed *the* milestone of their eighteen-year-old lives: graduating from Ocean View High. After two whirlwind weeks of finals, a fund-raising auction, the senior awards banquet, Senior Cut Day, the prom, and graduation itself, they were getting ready for what Ashley knew would be their best summer ever.

After all, this was the last summer before they all went their separate ways into the "Real World"—i.e., college. Ashley and Mary-Kate were going to the same college in New York City, although they wouldn't be rooming together. That was about as "separate" as they wanted to be!

In any case, Ashley planned to make the most of these next three months. She saw many beach parties, bonfires, and shopping sprees in her near future.

Of course, all this fun would cost major bucks, which was why she, Mary-Kate, and their two friends had lined up summer jobs. Ashley was seriously considering majoring in pre-law at college, and she knew her experience at Atwater, Bumble, and Chang—or *A-B-C*, as she was starting to think of it—was sure to help.

"Oops, I've gotta go." Mary-Kate suddenly jumped to her feet.

Claudia groaned. "But we just got started with our fashion show!"

"What's the matter, Mary-Kate? Got a hot date?" Felicity joked.

Mary-Kate blushed five shades of red.

Ashley knew exactly what that meant. "You *do* have a hot date!" she exclaimed. She got up and gave her sister a big hug. "Where's Trevor taking you?"

Mary-Kate turned even redder, if that was possible. "I'm not sure. Uh, someplace."

Trevor Reynolds had been Mary-Kate's best bud since forever. Everyone but the two of them had known that they were meant to be together as more than friends, though. During senior week they had finally figured it out, too. Tonight would be their first official date-date.

"Is it a beach date? You want to borrow one of our bikinis?" Claudia asked her. "You've got ten colors to choose from!"

"You are *not* touching my power suit," Ashley teased her sister.

Mary-Kate laughed as she headed for the door. "Thanks, guys, but I'm all set. I think it's a jeans and T-shirt kind of date."

"Have fun!" Felicity called out. "I'll keep my cell on in case you need advice. You know, like, if he gets a yucky piece of spinach stuck in his teeth, do you say something or not?"

"If he orders pesto, should you order pesto, too, so you both have garlic breath when he kisses you later?" Claudia added, wriggling her eyebrows.

Mary-Kate laughed again and disappeared down the hall.

Ashley could tell that her sister was beyond excited about this date, although she was trying her best to hide it. Ashley couldn't wait to get the full rundown when Mary-Kate got home.

"Ah, the first date," Claudia said with a sigh. "Is that romantic, or what? I so remember every single detail of my first date with Cooper." Cooper Firenz was her longtime boyfriend.

"I plan to have *lots* of first dates this summer,"

Felicity said, grinning. "How about you, Ashley?"

"Oh, I'm kind of first-dated-out," Ashley replied. In an effort to be more fun and spontaneous she had asked all sorts of guys out during senior week. Unfortunately, she had had some problems . . . juggling. The boys had all found out about one another and gotten mad at her. She was looking forward to taking a major time-out from dating for a while.

"Besides, there's more to life than guys," Ashley pointed out.

"Yeah, *right*," Felicity said, rolling her eyes.

"There is!" Ashley reached into a desk drawer and whipped out a fresh legal pad. She had a huge pile of them, all ready to go for her new job. "Come on, let's make a list. 'Top Ten Things to Do This Summer!'"

Claudia flopped down onto Ashley's bed. "Beach!" she exclaimed. "That should be number one."

"And beach *parties*," Felicity added.

Ashley began writing furiously. "Good, good. And let's not forget movie nights with manicures."

"Excellent add," Claudia said, nodding.

As Ashley scribbled away, she thought about how much fun the summer was going to be with Mary-Kate, Felicity, and Claudia. Senior summer only happened once in a lifetime. Ashley planned to make it a perfect blast!

Not only would she make money for the summer and college, but she would also get to mingle with lawyers who could help her learn the ropes. Maybe help her get into law school someday and—

The phone rang. Ashley picked it up. "Hello?"

"Ashley Olsen, please."

The unfamiliar-sounding male voice made Ashley sit up straighter. "This is Ashley."

"Good afternoon, Ms. Olsen. This is Ed Lindner from Atwater, Bumble, and Chang."

"If it's Cooper, tell him I'm not here!" Claudia called out. She and Felicity burst into a fit of giggles.

Ashley put a finger to her lips and shook her head fiercely. This was an important work call, and she didn't want to blow it.

"Oh, hi, Mr. Lindner. What can I do for you?" Ashley asked. She crossed her legs, flipped to a new page in her legal pad, and prepared to take notes. Even though her job wasn't starting for a whole week, they were already calling her! *This is too cool!*

"I'm afraid I have some bad news, Ms. Olsen. The partners just announced a new round of budget cuts. I'm afraid we won't be able to hire any interns this summer. That includes you," Mr. Lindner added.

Ashley froze. *Did he just say what I think he said?* she wondered. *Nah. No way. Maybe I'm just having a bad dream.*

"Ms. Olsen?" Mr. Lindner's voice cut into her thoughts. "We're all very sorry about this. We'll keep your résumé on file for next summer, of course."

Ashley managed to thank him and say good-bye before hanging up. Claudia and Felicity were both staring at her intently.

"Ash? What's up?" Felicity asked her worriedly.

"Earth to Ashley?" Claudia said, waving a hand in front of Ashley's face.

Ashley took a deep breath and said, "I think I just got fired."

The doorbell rang. Mary-Kate felt a rush of panic. Trevor was four minutes early!

"I am *so* not ready for this," she said under her breath.

She headed down the stairs, praying that she didn't look like a complete troll. She was wearing her fourth-favorite choice of top with her jeans because the first three had been in the laundry. She had accidentally used the wrong kind of hair gel, and her blond hair was sticking out in funny places despite her best efforts to tame it. She had checked and rechecked to make sure she didn't have candy-pink lip gloss on her teeth—but what if she had missed a spot?

The doorbell rang again.

"Mary-Kate? Ashley?" her mother called from the kitchen. "Can one of you girls get that?"

"I've got it, Mom!" Mary-Kate yelled back.

As Mary-Kate neared the front door, she realized that her heart was racing a million miles a minute. Her palms were sweaty, too. *Why?* she wondered. *It's only Trevor.*

Only Trevor. Mary-Kate felt her cheeks flush and her lips curl up into a happy smile. *Only Trevor* had turned into so much more during graduation week. He had told her what she had been waiting to hear for years—that he thought of her as way more than a friend. Now they were going on their first real date.

And Mary-Kate had never been more nervous in her life.

She checked her appearance one last time in the hall mirror. Okay, so maybe she didn't look like a *total* troll. She took a slow, deep, calming breath and opened the front door.

Her breath caught in her throat. Trevor was standing there, looking—well—*amazing.* His usually choppy brown hair was styled ever so slightly so that it stood up in subtle spikes. His supercute face was smooth and clean-shaven and infinitely kissable.

Mary-Kate's gaze wandered—and froze.

Trevor was wearing a suit and tie! And here she was, dressed in her favorite faded jeans and her not-so-favorite tank top.

"You look so . . . and I look so . . . um . . . let me go change," Mary-Kate found herself sputtering.

With one hand behind his back, Trevor smiled and put his other hand on her shoulder. Mary-Kate felt tingly where he touched her.

"You look great," he said, his dark brown eyes taking her in. "Don't change. You look perfect just like that."

Mary-Kate's cheeks were positively on fire now. His compliment had completely unhinged her. She could barely bring herself to look him in the eye.

"Thank you," she whispered. "That's really—um, thank you."

Mary-Kate knew she sounded lame. She couldn't help it, though. Trevor had that effect on her.

Trevor blushed and grinned. It was almost as though he knew exactly what she was feeling inside and was feeling it, too.

Then he produced a daisy from behind his back. "For you," he said simply. "I hope you like it."

"Oh, that's so sweet!" Mary-Kate said, surprised. She lifted the daisy to her face and inhaled its delicate fragrance. "Oh, wow. Thank you so much."

"You're welcome. I tried to find a rose, but they were all out."

"Hey, I'm a daisy kind of girl anyway."

"You sure are." Trevor offered her his arm. "Ready?"

Mary-Kate giggled and threaded her arm through his. He was acting like such a gentleman. She knew it wouldn't last, that soon they'd be back to their usual teasing, but it was still fun. "Yes, definitely!"

As they headed outside to Trevor's Jeep Wrangler, Mary-Kate glanced up at the sunset sky streaked with pink and gold, the first hint of a star shining on the horizon. The date had just barely started, and it was already perfect.

Trevor held the passenger door open for her. As she began to sit down, she felt something crunch underneath her.

"Oh, sorry," Trevor apologized as she stood up again. He reached into the car and pulled out a bag of potato chips. "Lunch," he explained.

"No problem," Mary-Kate said. She glanced at the seat to make sure it was all clear, then sat down and kicked away some wrappers on the floor. So much for the gentleman act. She should have remembered that the inside of Trevor's car was usually a minefield. She was glad things were really still the same.

Trevor slid into the driver's seat and started the car. "Okay?" he asked her.

"Absolutely." Mary-Kate smiled.

Mary-Kate dipped a tortilla into a bowl of yummy guacamole and glanced around the crowded restaurant. Trevor had brought her to El Sol, a brand-new Mexican place right on the beach. The décor consisted of dark brown walls and mismatched tables painted with burnt-orange and turquoise designs. Strings of tiny white lights blinked from cactus plants and miniature palm trees. Dozens of candles cast a hazy golden glow around the room. Mary-Kate could smell the sea breeze in the air.

"So, I have a big announcement to make," Trevor said, leaning forward.

"You're going to order chicken burritos instead of veggie burritos?" she teased.

Trevor gave her a playful smack on the arm. "Ha! I don't think so. I've got a job," he said.

"You do? Where?" Mary-Kate knew that Trevor had applied to at least half a dozen places for the summer: a bookstore, a record store, a bike shop, a weekly newspaper, and more. So far the news had all been bad. All the jobs had already been taken.

Trevor took a sip of his coconut-pineapple smoothie and wriggled his eyebrows. "Starts with an *S*," he hinted.

"Wow, that's really helpful." Mary-Kate grinned. "*S, S, S* . . . the Sunset Café?"

"Nope."

"Surf's Up?"

"Uh-uh."

"Sadie's Sandwich Shoppe?"

"You're getting warmer!" Trevor encouraged her.

"I am? Hmm, is it Arnold's Deli?"

"No, Mary-Kate, remember the *S*! Actually, the initials are *S-S-S*. What has the initials *S-S-S*?"

What was Trevor talking about?

And then it came to her. Her heart did a somersault in her chest. "Oh, no *way*," she said in a voice barely above a whisper.

Trevor gave her a huge smile, his eyes twinkling. "Way. You're looking at a future employee of the Silver Spurs Stables."

Mary-Kate jumped up to give him a hug, trying not to knock all the dishes off the table as she did so. Then she drew back and punched him on the arm. He punched her back, then started tickling her. This was their ritual from when they were friends, and it was a hard habit to break.

After getting some funny looks from the other customers, Mary-Kate made herself sit down.

Trevor stared at her with a pleased expression. "So, this is good news?"

"This is *great* news," Mary-Kate replied, running a hand through her hair to smooth it into place. "I didn't even know you were applying there."

"I kind of wanted to surprise you," Trevor admitted. "I saw their ad in the paper last week. At first I wasn't going to apply, because I didn't want you to feel . . . well, you know, that I was crowding you or whatever. But then I thought, why not?"

"Wow," Mary-Kate said, stunned and happy.

Trevor looked at her intently. "So it's okay? You like the idea of our working together this summer?" He sounded nervous.

Mary-Kate reached across the table and squeezed his hand. "It's *totally* okay," she replied.

Trevor smiled. "Cool."

The waiter came by just then and set down two plates of steaming food. "Veggie burritos with rice and beans. Shrimp quesadillas with extra guacamole," he announced.

"That's mine," Mary-Kate said, pointing to the quesadillas. "Although we can totally share," she added to Trevor.

"Definitely," Trevor said, grinning. "Thumbs-up to sharing."

As they plunged into the delicious food, Mary-Kate and Trevor talked about the stables. Mary-Kate liked how everything was so easy, so natural between them. And yet at the same time Trevor made her heart beat faster and her palms feel all sweaty. She even loved the tiny glob of salsa on his cheek. He'd always been a supermessy eater. It used to bug her, but now it just seemed sweet.

Is this what love feels like? Mary-Kate wondered.

After El Sol, Trevor brought Mary-Kate to a secluded spot on the beach. He laid his jacket down on the sand, and they sat down.

Off in the distance Mary-Kate could see the bright lights of the restaurants and cafés in town. But here she and Trevor were alone—completely alone.

They had talked and talked at the restaurant— about graduation, about the summer, about the student handbook Mary-Kate and Ashley had just received from Lawton College, about the tour Trevor had taken of his new art school, about everything. Now they were both still and quiet.

Moonlight shimmered on the waves as they rolled in, then gently receded. Mary-Kate snuggled closer to Trevor. He wrapped an arm around her shoulders.

"You cold?" he whispered into her ear.

"Not anymore," she whispered back.

She was so happy and nervous and excited, she could barely breathe.

But I've known him forever, she thought.

She knew what Ashley would say if she told her that: *Not like this.*

Trevor's voice broke into her thoughts. "I have a surprise for you."

"*Another* one?" Mary-Kate said, incredulous.

"This one's different."

Trevor reached into his jacket pocket and pulled out a small box. It was wrapped in the Sunday comics.

Mary-Kate's jaw dropped. "W-what's that?" she stammered.

"It's kind of a late graduation present," Trevor replied. "I hope you like it."

Mary-Kate instantly felt guilty. "But I don't have a graduation present for you," she said apologetically.

"Don't worry about it. Just open the box," Trevor said, nudging the package into her hands. "Sorry about the wrapping. I kind of forgot to buy some."

"No problem. Remember the time you gave me a

CD for my birthday and wrapped it in a paper towel?" Mary-Kate reminded him.

Trevor laughed. "Oh, yeah."

Mary-Kate took the box from him and began unwrapping it. She couldn't wait to see what was inside. Earrings? A choker? A cool new key chain for her car keys?

Underneath the wrapping was a simple white box. Mary-Kate opened it—and gasped.

Inside was a silver charm bracelet with a single heart-shaped charm on it.

"Omigosh," Mary-Kate whispered. "It's *beautiful*!"

"Really? You like it?" Trevor asked her eagerly.

Mary-Kate sighed. "I *love* it."

Trevor fingered the charm. "I didn't have the charm engraved. I wasn't sure exactly what to say." He gave her a shy smile and added, "By the end of the summer I'll know. I'll have it engraved for you then."

Mary-Kate felt butterflies in her stomach. Trevor was the sweetest guy in the world. And not only was he her best friend, but now he was her boyfriend, too.

He hadn't actually said that word yet: *boyfriend*. But he was acting like a boyfriend. The charm bracelet clinched it.

Trevor put the bracelet onto her left wrist. His face was really close to hers as he struggled to hook the tiny clasp. "Got it," he said, securing the catch.

He didn't pull away. Instead he took Mary-Kate's

face in both his hands. Her heart hammered in her chest as his lips moved toward hers ever so slowly. When he kissed her, she felt as though fireworks were going off in her head.

There will never be another first date like this, she thought. *Ever.*

AshleyO invites Claude18 and Felicity_girl to Instant Message!

AshleyO: I cd flip burgers at the Burgerplex.

Felicity_girl: grease is bad 4 complexion.

Claude18: how bout mall?

AshleyO: I cd pierce ears at World of Pain.

Felicity_girl: Free earrings, yes!

AshleyO: Or park cars at Mega-Dome lot.

Claude18: Stand in hot sun for 8 hours waving at cars?

Felicity_girl: YUCK!!!

AshleyO: This is hard. Is it 2 late 2 go back 2 high school?

CHAPTER TWO

Ashley pointed the remote at the television set. *Click*. An exercise show for pregnant moms and their pets. *Click*. An old, old rerun of *Next Generation*. *Click*. How to make meatless meat loaf. *Click*. A 1960s movie about killer pigeons invading Detroit. *Click*.

As usual Ashley pondered the irony that even though her family subscribed to a zillion cable stations, there was nothing on. She slunk down deeper on the couch and dug into the bowl of her favorite microwave popcorn, which was fat-free and nacho-flavored.

A documentary about breeding show dogs. *Click*.

She should have been out christening the beginning of the summer with Felicity and Claudia, who had gone to see a late showing of the new Jude Law movie at the mall. Instead she was sitting at home in her jams and stewing.

How could Atwater, Bumble, and Chang fire her before she had even started working there? Okay, well, maybe not *fire* her, exactly, but let her go?

She had totally not been up to seeing a movie at the

mall. Instead she had gone through all the want ads in all the local newspapers, plus searched online through hundreds of listings. Ashley recalled Mary-Kate saying that Trevor was having problems finding a job. All the prime summer jobs seemed to have been taken already.

Of course, it *was* summer already. Only the unlucky ones like her had been left in the dust.

Ashley sighed. She wished Mary-Kate would come home from her date. She had to tell her sister the awful news about her nipped-in-the-bud legal career. Mary-Kate would know what to do. And even if she didn't, she would help Ashley drown her sorrows in a pint of mint-chocolate-chip frozen yogurt.

Just then Ashley heard noises on the front porch: footsteps, the jingling of keys. It was Mary-Kate. *Yes!* she thought, jumping off the couch and heading for the front door. *Help has arrived!*

Ashley heard the low murmur of voices coming from outside. She peeked through the keyhole. It *was* Mary-Kate—and Trevor. Their lips were locked in a major good-night kiss.

"Oops!" Ashley muttered under her breath.

She ran back to the couch. She clicked on the television set and picked up a random magazine from the coffee table, trying to look busy.

The front door opened, and Mary-Kate walked in. "Hey, Ashley," she called out in a breathless-sounding voice. "You still up?"

Ashley glanced over her shoulder. "Oh, I was just chilling," she replied casually. "Did you have a good time?"

"Yes!" Mary-Kate exclaimed. She came over to the couch and sat down next to Ashley. "Yes, yes, yes! It was *perfect.*"

Ashley saw that her sister's face was glowing and radiant. *Love—it's better than makeup,* she thought.

"I'm really happy for you," Ashley said, meaning it. "What was he wearing? Where did he take you? And why do you have sand all over your jeans?"

Mary-Kate stared at Ashley. "Before I answer all your questions, I have one for you. Why are you reading that magazine upside down?"

"Huh?" Ashley hastily flipped her copy of *People* right side up. "Oh! I was, um, just, um, checking out what Nicole Kidman's dress would look like from a different angle."

"And what are you watching on TV? It looks like a poodle fashion show," Mary-Kate said, puzzled.

Ashley sighed and clicked the television off. "Okay, I'm busted," she admitted. "I've been waiting up for you so I could break the bad news."

"Bad news? What is it?" Mary-Kate demanded.

"Atwater, Bumble, and Chang. Budget cuts. Job cuts. You get the picture," Ashley replied.

Mary-Kate gasped. "Oh, no! When did you find out?"

"Just after you left on your date with Trevor,"

Ashley said. "Felicity and Claudia offered to cheer me up with a home pedicure. But I was too depressed to care about smooth feet, you know?"

"I know," Mary-Kate said, nodding with mock seriousness. "Sometimes dry skin just doesn't seem important next to *real* issues."

"So they took off to see the new Jude Law movie."

Mary-Kate reached over and gave Ashley a big reassuring hug. "It's going to be okay. We'll just have to find you another job." Her eyes lit up. "Hey! What about the Silver Spurs Stables? Trevor just got a job there. I think he said there might be other openings. Maybe I could talk to the director for you."

"Trevor's working with you at the stables this summer? You lucky girl," Ashley said. Then she grinned and shook her head. "Thanks, but no thanks. I think I'd feel like a third wheel."

"You would not be a third wheel," Mary-Kate insisted loyally.

"You're in love. You're not objective." Ashley pointed to Mary-Kate's wrist. "Hey, where'd you get that bracelet? I've never seen it before."

Mary-Kate smiled and blushed. "Trevor gave it to me. It's a graduation present."

Ashley touched the small silver heart charm dangling from the chain. "Wow, that's beautiful."

"He gave it to me on the beach," Mary-Kate said, her eyes sparkling.

"That is so romantic," Ashley agreed. Now, it was *her* turn to give her sister a hug. "I am totally happy for you. So *that's* why you have sand on your jeans. You and Trevor were having a lovefest on the beach."

Then Ashley sat straight up. *"Beach,"* she repeated. "That's it!"

Mary-Kate frowned. "Huh?"

Ashley grinned. "I just thought of another couple who wouldn't mind having a third wheel around. A couple of *friends,* that is."

Ashley sat across the desk from Nico Montero, the owner and manager of the Caribe Beach Club. Nico was on the phone yelling at someone.

Ashley tried not to stare at Nico too much while he yelled. But she couldn't help it. For one thing, he had a really . . . *unusual* appearance. His hair was thick and jet black and came down to his waist. And he had the longest, funkiest-looking toenails she'd ever seen. *Yuck.*

"I need those beach towels, and I need them now!" Nico shouted to the person on the other end of the phone. "What kind of operation do you run over there anyway?"

He hung up abruptly and turned to Ashley. "Now, what can I do for you? Audrey, right?"

Ashley smiled nervously. "Actually, it's Ashley."

"Right, *Ashley*! Claudia and Felicity recommended

you. They said you wanted to apply for a job here."

Ashley nodded. "That's right!"

Nico began shuffling through a massive pile of papers on his desk. "Now, Ashley, I don't mean to be negative right off the bat, but isn't this kind of last-minute for you to be applying for a summer job? This says to me you have a problem with procrastination. You know what that means, *pro-cras-ti-na-tion*?" He emphasized each syllable.

Before Ashley could reply, she felt something soft and feathery brush the back of her neck. She jumped in her chair. "Wh–what was that?" she asked, startled.

"Oh, that's Mrs. Caldwell," Nico replied, waving a hand dismissively. "Just ignore her."

Ashley turned around. A large blue and white parrot was flying through the room. It circled twice, then landed on a wooden perch above a filing cabinet.

"Just ignore her! Just ignore her!" the parrot squawked.

"Back to your procrastination problem," Nico prompted Ashley.

"Procrastination problem! Procrastination problem!" the parrot shrieked.

Ashley turned back to face Nico. She was having a hard time focusing with Mrs. Caldwell in the room.

"Um . . . that is . . . I don't have a procrastination problem," Ashley said to Nico. "Just the opposite. All my teachers say I'm superorganized. The reason I'm applying so late is because I had another job lined up, and it fell through due to budget cuts. At a law firm," she added. "Atwater, Bumble, and Chang."

"Atwater, Bumble, and Chang!" the parrot repeated.

"A law firm," Nico repeated, looking suspicious. "If you're interested in law, why are you looking for work at my beach club? Isn't that a step down for you?"

Boy, this guy is tough, Ashley thought. Out loud she said, "A job at a law firm was my first choice for this summer. But the most important thing is that I work hard and save money for college." *And clothes and CDs,* she added silently.

"Money for college!" said the parrot, fixing her gaze on Ashley.

Nico leaned across his cluttered desk and frowned at Ashley. At that moment, with his beady brown eyes, he looked almost like his parrot.

"Are you telling me that you're going to be happy making smoothies instead of, you know, schmoozing with the suits?" Nico asked her pointedly.

Ashley nodded. "Definitely!"

"Definitely!" the parrot echoed.

Nico shuffled some more papers. Ashley's heart plummeted. This interview was going nowhere. No way was she going to get this job.

Ashley picked her backpack off the floor and zipped it up, preparing to go. Then Nico mumbled something.

"I'm sorry, I didn't hear you," Ashley said.

"You've got the job, Ashley! You've got the job, Ashley!" the parrot squawked.

Ashley couldn't believe it. She grinned at Nico. "Really?"

"Yeah, really. You start on Monday, 9:00 A.M. sharp. I'm putting you on smoothie duty. But I'm keeping my eye on you, kid," Nico warned her.

Kid? she thought. *What movie is he stuck in?* "Thank you, Mr. Montero. Thank you, Mrs. Caldwell. See you Monday!" Ashley said eagerly.

She picked up her backpack and rushed outside into the bright, sunny day. She couldn't wait to tell Felicity and Claudia the good news. Now the three of them would be able to spend almost every day together, making smoothies, fetching towels, and checking out cute guys.

This summer might not be going exactly as she'd planned. But it was going to be even *better*!

AshleyO invites Mary★★★Kate, Felicity_girl, and Claude18 to Instant Message!

AshleyO: I got the job! I got the job!

Mary★★★Kate: YES!!!

Felicity_girl: We knew U cd do it!:)

Claude18: Fel and me will have 2 take U
bikini shopping.

AshleyO: BTW, whats up with the freak
parrot?

Felicity_girl: Dont ask.

Claude18: Ash, this is awesome news.
The three of us will rule the beach
club!

Mary★★★Kate: I wish it cd B the 4 of
us!

AshleyO: Ditto. But U get Trev!

Mary★★★Kate: True.

Felicity_girl: This is all very
Xcellent. This summer's gonna rule!

CHAPTER THREE

Mary-Kate stood under a eucalyptus tree at the edge of the paddock and watched the walkers warming up the horses. It was a beautiful day, without a single cloud in the sky. The horses made gentle whinnying noises and kicked up clouds of reddish-brown dust as they moved. Juniper and piñon trees swayed in the warm breeze. From her vantage point on top of the Hollywood Hills, Mary-Kate could see the vast landscape of Los Angeles down below.

"Olsen! You're on mucking duty today! Stable number four!"

Mary-Kate turned to see Terri Foster, the owner of the Silver Spurs Stables. She was a petite woman with short blond hair, intense green eyes, and muscles to die for. *Working with horses is obviously right up there with weight lifting and Pilates*, Mary-Kate thought with admiration.

"I'll get started right away, Ms. Foster," Mary-Kate replied. She hurried off in the direction of the stables.

It was almost noon, and the sun was high in the

sky. The morning of Mary-Kate's first day on the job—everyone's first day on the job—had been taken up with a long, comprehensive orientation filled with rules and regs. The summer employees had also gotten the lowdown on their various duties, such as leading kids on trail rides, grooming horses, cleaning stables, and more.

Trevor was on trail duty today. Mary-Kate had seen him during orientation, across the sea of faces. She had tried not to stare at him too much, but that had been difficult. He had spent a lot of time staring at her, too—and also assuming various goofy expressions that made her crack up.

They had agreed to meet for lunch later on. Mary-Kate couldn't wait. She had already picked out the perfect picnic spot under a shady palm tree.

She soon reached a row of big brown barns and headed for the one marked #4. Inside, two girls were busily cleaning out stalls. One of them had long, curly black hair pulled back in a ponytail and caramel-colored skin. She was wearing jeans and a red T-shirt with a big yellow smiley face on it. The other girl was tall and slim with short auburn hair. She wore a T-shirt with hearts all over it.

"Hi there!" the dark-haired girl called out to Mary-Kate in a friendly voice. "Did Boss Lady put you on mucking duty, too?"

"Yup," Mary-Kate said. She reached for a rake and

a shovel hanging on the wall. "Looks like fun!" she joked.

"Totally *not*," the girl replied. "I'm Aisha."

"I'm Danielle," the other girl said.

"Your name is Mary-something, right?" Aisha asked.

"Mary-Kate."

Aisha ran a hand across her forehead, wiping away dirt and sweat. "Oh, right, Mary-Kate. I hope we don't get you mixed up with the other two Mary-somethings. Mary-Beth and Mary-Louise. Do you know them? Mary-Beth is the one with the long red hair. She's dating one of the stablehands, Fernando. Mary-Louise *used* to date Fernando, until he broke up with her to date Mary-Beth. Is that weird, or what? He must have a thing for girls named Mary-something. Hey, maybe he'll want to go out with you next!" Aisha cracked up.

Mary-Kate chuckled politely. Aisha seemed to know everyone.

"Actually, I feel sorry for Fernando," Danielle piped up. "He's a really spiritual person. He told me all about his breakup with Mary-Louise. He said she didn't respect his Capricorn nature."

"Oh, brother." Aisha groaned.

As the two girls chattered on about Fernando's love life, Mary-Kate walked to an empty stall. She kicked some hay aside and started shoveling horse manure into a large bucket. The smell was really awful. But she tried to tell herself that it smelled *good,* like rolling meadows and farms.

Rolling meadows and farms, rolling meadows and farms, she chanted in her head. But the chant didn't seem to work. She wished she had a pair of nose plugs instead.

"Have you met anyone else here?" Danielle asked Mary-Kate.

"Well, I kind of know some people from school," Mary-Kate replied vaguely, continuing to shovel. For some reason she didn't want to spill the beans about her relationship with Trevor just yet. It was still new and special to her, and she didn't want the girls to see how flustered she could get just talking about him. "How about you guys?"

"Oh, we know *everyone,*" Aisha said with a grin. "We worked here last summer. A lot of the other kids did, too. Like, have you met Daria and Will? They were a major item here last summer. But this year—*forget* about it! She has a new boyfriend at school, some basketball player. Will's still not over her, though. He's in looooove!"

"Will doesn't *deserve* Daria," Danielle remarked. "Do you know what he did? He got her a Miners CD for her birthday. The Miners are so last month!"

"That's no reason to dump him for a basketball player," Aisha pointed out.

"Of course it is!"

Aisha and Danielle continued gossiping about other couples and ex-couples at the Silver Spurs Stables. As Mary-Kate listened and mucked, she started getting a queasy feeling about telling Aisha and Danielle—telling *anyone* here—about her and Trevor. Did every Silver Spurs couple get microanalyzed this way?

Mary-Kate's thoughts were interrupted by Aisha's voice. "I gotta get a soda. Who wants a soda?"

"I'll go with you," Danielle offered. "I need a fresh-air break." She waved a hand in front of her nose, and they all laughed.

"I'm all set, thanks," Mary-Kate replied.

Aisha and Danielle took off. Mary-Kate finished up with her stall and began working on another one. *Rolling meadows and farms, rolling meadows and farms,* she kept telling herself, trying to get used to the smell. She couldn't wait till she was assigned trail duty or even grooming duty—anything that was a little less *fragrant*.

"Hey."

Mary-Kate stopped what she was doing and turned around. Trevor was standing there, smiling at her.

"What are you doing here?" Mary-Kate asked with surprise. She was filled with happiness and panic at the same time—happiness because Trevor had come to see her, and panic because she was knee-deep in horse manure.

Is he still going to like me when I'm this gross and smelly? she wondered.

31

"I'm on a break," Trevor replied, moving closer. "I wanted to say hi."

"Hey." Mary-Kate noticed how cute Trevor looked in his riding pants and denim shirt.

"How's it going?" Trevor asked her. "Looks like hard work."

"It is. Don't come close to me. I'm really, really disgusting," Mary-Kate insisted.

"You could *never* be disgusting, Mary-Kate," Trevor said sweetly, still wading through the hay toward her.

Mary-Kate grinned. "What about the time I was covered with poison ivy? From our hike?"

Trevor made a face. "Oh, yeah. You *were* pretty disgusting then."

Mary-Kate laughed and punched his arm. "Troll!"

"Freak!"

Mary-Kate stopped laughing and glanced around. "By the way," she said in a low voice, "I think we need to be careful around here."

Trevor frowned. "What do you mean?"

Mary-Kate told Trevor about Aisha and Danielle's endless gossip. "I think we should be careful about our relationship, or everyone will be talking about us, too," she finished.

"I don't know. Doesn't matter to me." Trevor looked thoughtful, then grinned. "On the other hand, it might be kinda fun sneaking around."

Mary-Kate smiled. "*Sneaking around?* As in, acting as if we're just acquaintances?"

"In public, yeah," Trevor replied. "But in private . . ."

He pulled Mary-Kate into his arms and kissed her on the lips. "See what I mean?" he said when they came up for air.

"I see what you mean," Mary-Kate agreed, feeling dizzy and warm all over. "I'm sorry I'm so disgusting."

"You are totally *not* disgusting."

"Okay, then do that again."

Trevor laughed and kissed her again.

"Mary-Kate?" a familiar voice called out. "We've got snacks!"

Yikes! It was Aisha and Danielle! Without wasting a second, Mary-Kate pushed herself out of Trevor's arms.

She put on her best mean face. "There's no way I'm going to work a double shift to cover for you next Monday," she said loudly. "Try your line on someone else!"

Trevor looked confused for a moment, then seemed to catch on. "Fine, whatever. I just thought I'd ask."

Aisha and Danielle walked in. Aisha glanced at Trevor, then at Mary-Kate. "Sorry, are we interrupting?" she asked obviously.

Danielle made a beeline for Trevor. "Hi, I'm Danielle," she said, smiling at him. "Are you new here? What are you doing for lunch?"

Hey, back off! He's having lunch with me! Mary-Kate wanted to say. But she bit her lip and willed herself to stay silent.

"Uh, thanks, but I have plans. See you later," Trevor said to Danielle. Then, out of Danielle and Aisha's view, Trevor winked at Mary-Kate. She had to resist the impulse to wink back. Then he took off down the trail, whistling a song under his breath.

"What a jerk," Mary-Kate said to Aisha.

"Yeah, but what a *cute* jerk," Danielle replied, staring after him. "What's his name?"

Mary-Kate took a deep breath and shrugged. "Travis. Ted. Who knows? Who cares?"

"Hey, did I tell you about this guy named Travis who worked here last summer?" Aisha asked. She picked up her shovel and started babbling about Travis and his many girlfriends. Danielle joined in.

Mary-Kate half-listened, thinking about the happy secret Trevor and she shared. The more she thought about it, the more it sounded fun to keep it a secret.

As long as Danielle and all the other girls at Silver Spurs keep their hands off Trevor, that is.

"Would you like peach, strawberry, blueberry, raspberry, or the superspecial combo?"

Ashley smiled at the guy who was standing on the other side of the counter. He smiled back at her. She could tell that he was admiring the way she looked in her new pink bikini and matching pink-and-yellow sarong.

"Which one's *your* favorite?" the guy asked her.

"The superspecial combo, definitely. It has a little of everything," Ashley said.

"That's what I'll take, then. The extra-large size. And keep the change." The guy put a ten-dollar bill on the counter.

"Thank you!"

There was a long line of people behind him. Ashley's smoothie stand was a big success. It was only her first day, and already she had raked in about forty dollars in tips.

As she hit the ON button on the blender and watched the chunks of fresh fruit liquefy, she thanked her lucky stars for this job. If one could *call* it a job, that was. She got to hang out on a gorgeous beach all day long. She got to make smoothies, which she considered to be the perfect archetypal food form. She got to work with two of her best buds, Felicity and Claudia. She also got to check out cute guys and have fun. And she got *paid* for it!

The next two customers in line were a pair of teenaged girls. "Two strawberry smoothies, please. Medium," the first girl said, then turned back to the other girl. "So he says he's got a game, but he'll call me on his cell afterward about where to meet," she complained. "The thing is, I don't have a cell phone. My parents won't let me have one because they're total dictators. That means I have to wait at home for him to call me just to figure out where we're going to *meet*."

"That is so lame," the other girl agreed.

Ashley listened to the two girls talk while she mixed up the strawberry smoothies. "Listen," she said after a minute. "Maybe this is none of my business, but I have one thing to say about cell-phone dating."

The two girls stopped talking and looked at her. "What?" asked the first girl.

"Don't go there," Ashley advised. "If a guy wants to go out with you, he should agree with you ahead of time about the time and the place. For him to keep you waiting by the phone is totally disrespectful."

The first girl looked at her friend. "She's right," she said.

"Totally," the other girl agreed. "You're smart!"

"Thanks!" the first girl said to Ashley.

Ashley handed them their smoothies. "No problem!" she said, grinning. "Next!"

Ashley had twenty more customers before her lunch break. Just before noon Felicity and Claudia came wandering over. They both looked stunning in their matching bikinis and sarongs. Felicity had been handing out towels all morning, while Claudia was checking beach tags.

"Yo, Ash," Felicity said, waving. "Ready for some sustenance?"

"How did your first morning go?" Claudia asked her, adjusting her shades.

Ashley smiled and gave the thumbs-up. "Great. Perfect! Actually, I'm *happy* A, B, and C fired me."

Felicity laughed. "That's the spirit!"

"I love working here. I love the beach. And I love hanging out with you guys!" Ashley said, wrapping her arms around her friends' shoulders. "We are going to have the most awesome summer together."

"Beach all day, party all night!" Claudia sang.

A cell phone rang. It was a tinny version of the national anthem.

"Oops! That's me," Felicity said. She reached into her beach tote and pulled out a tiny pink phone. "Hello? Oh, hey, Dad."

Felicity fell silent. Ashley watched her friend's face as she listened to her father. Something was up. Felicity's eyes were getting so big, they were practically bugging out of her head.

"Omigosh," Felicity said finally. *"OMIGOSH!"*

"What? *What?*" Claudia demanded.

"What's going on?" Ashley asked.

"I'll talk to you later, okay, Dad? I'll call you after lunch. Thanks!" Felicity squealed.

She clicked off her cell phone and turned to Ashley and Claudia. "Guess what!" she screeched. Some of the customers turned to stare at her. "Dad just found out that he's going to Spain for a month! On a business trip! He's leaving Monday!"

"Great. So you'll get a lot of cool souvenirs and a

little less parental supervision," Ashley pointed out. She still didn't understand why Felicity was acting so spastic.

Felicity shook her head. "Girlfriend, you don't understand! He said I can go *with* him. And he said I can bring a friend with me!"

"Omigosh!" Claudia screeched.

"Omigosh!" Ashley echoed.

Felicity grabbed Ashley and Claudia in a big group hug and began dancing around and around in a circle. Ashley felt happy and a little stunned at the same time. She was happy for Felicity, but she was also in shock because suddenly the summer wasn't going to be the same anymore. Felicity would be away for an entire month!

And then something else occurred to Ashley. Felicity was allowed to bring one friend with her to Spain. Just one.

Who was it going to be?

Felicity_girl invites AshleyO to Instant Message!

Felicity_girl: Hey, girlfriend. So I've
  been thinking.
AshleyO: Don't wear yourself out.
Felicity_girl: Ha ha! I get to bring 1
  friend 2 Spain. Do U want 2 go?
AshleyO: Omigosh. Oh, wow. Well. Hmm.
Felicity_girl: Is that a yes?
AshleyO: I really WANT 2 go :-(
Felicity_girl: But?
AshleyO: But I shd probably say no.
  I really need to make $ this summer.
Felicity_girl: You're so virtuous.
  I guess it's Claudia, then.
AshleyO: Yeah. I'm gonna miss you guys
  this summer!
Felicity_girl: Me, 2. But change is good.
AshleyO: Maybe. I hope so.

CHAPTER FOUR

Mary-Kate held the lead tightly in her hand and guided the stubborn horse around a bend in the path.

"Come on, Fred," she coaxed him, tugging on the lead. "This way. No, not *that* way."

"Is this horse dangerous?" asked the ten-year-old boy who was riding him.

"No, no, he's not dangerous at all. He's friendly! Come on, Fred," Mary-Kate urged.

Mary-Kate had had no idea that handling horses could be so tough. Her arm muscles hurt from keeping Fred under control.

"Is this your first day working here?" the boy asked.

This kid is too smart for his own good, Mary-Kate thought. "Definitely not," she replied. This was her *third* day at the Silver Spurs Stables. "Just relax," she instructed the boy. "A horse can pick up on your mood. If you're relaxed, he's relaxed. If you're nervous, he's nervous."

Mary-Kate wasn't sure this was true, but it sounded good.

"Really?" the boy asked her, his eyes wide.

"Really," Mary-Kate assured him. "So take a deep breath and think calm thoughts."

"Okay!"

The boy began exhaling loudly. Mary-Kate glanced over her shoulder to see who was behind her. Aisha was coming up the trail, leading a girl on a gray horse. Mary-Kate waved.

"Hey!" Aisha waved back. "How's it going?"

"Fred and I are doing great," Mary-Kate called out. "How's it going with you?"

Aisha hurried her steps until she and her horse and rider were right behind Mary-Kate. "Awesome," she replied. She lowered her voice and added, "Hey, guess what I just found out!"

More gossip, Mary-Kate thought, amused. "What?"

"Forget about Fernando, and forget about Travis. All the girls here are after a major new hottie," Aisha confided.

"What's a hottie?" the boy on Mary-Kate's horse asked.

"Never mind," Mary-Kate told him. "Keep breathing! Who is it?" she asked Aisha, curious.

"Remember that guy you were arguing with in the barn the other day?" Aisha said. "His name is Trevor Reynolds. He's single. He's hot. And he's like Silver Spurs Stables' 'Most Eligible Guy'!"

Mary-Kate stopped so abruptly that Aisha's horse

almost ran into Fred. *"What?"* Mary-Kate demanded.

Trevor is not *eligible. He's mine!* she wanted to scream. It took every ounce of her self-control to keep her mouth shut.

"I know you think he's rude, or whatever, but he's totally not. He's really sweet. *And* he looks like Ben Affleck," Aisha said, wriggling her eyebrows.

"Who's Ben Affleck?" the little girl on Aisha's horse asked.

This is a nightmare, Mary-Kate thought.

The woods ended, and the trail opened up into a clearing. Mary-Kate spotted Trevor up ahead, walking a horse across the paddocks. Her heart skipped a beat. He looked superhunky today in his faded jeans and black T-shirt. He was wearing a black baseball cap over his brown hair.

Just then Mary-Kate spotted a girl walking up to him. The girl put a hand on his arm. Then she looked up at him, said something, and giggled. Danielle!

Mary-Kate bit her lower lip. *Self-control,* she reminded herself.

Maybe this sneaking-around business isn't such a good idea after all.

"What do you think of Guava Pink? Or should I go for Lavender Starship today?" Ashley asked Mary-Kate.

The two of them were sitting in side-by-side manicure chairs at the Attitude Salon. It was Wednesday night, the night Ashley, Mary-Kate, Felicity, and Claudia had designated as their weekly girls' manicure night.

Except that Felicity and Claudia were late. Ashley twisted her left hand, which was soaking in a bowl of warm, soapy, rose-scented water, to glance at her watch. They should have been here twenty minutes ago. She wondered what was keeping them.

"Lavender Starship, definitely," Mary-Kate replied. "You did Guava Pink last week." She giggled and added, "I so need a manicure after cleaning out stalls!"

"Hey, I feel your pain. I broke two nails chopping up ice today," Ashley sympathized.

"How's your new job going?" Mary-Kate asked her.

"I *love* it," Ashley said, meaning it. "I get to make smoothies and gab with customers all day. On the *beach*. As far as I'm concerned, it's the perfect job!"

"Cool," Mary-Kate said.

"The best part is getting to hang out with Felicity and Claudia all the time," Ashley went on. She frowned. "Oh. Except now they're going to Spain. Things won't be the same without them!"

"I am *so jealous* they're going to Spain," Mary-Kate said. "I've heard they have supercool clubs there."

"And cute guys, too," Ashley added.

Mary-Kate giggled. "Not as cute as Trevor."

"Yeah, like you're real objective," Ashley teased her. Then she spotted Felicity and Claudia sauntering into the salon. They were walking arm in arm, their heads bent together, laughing about something. They were loaded down with shopping bags.

"Hey, you freaks! You're late!" Mary-Kate called out to them.

"Yeah, they ran out of nail polish!" Ashley joked.

Felicity sat down in an empty manicure chair next to Ashley and crossed her legs. "Ha ha, very funny. We don't have time for manicures anyway."

"No time for manicures? What kind of crazy talk is that?" Mary-Kate demanded.

"Too busy shopping for travel clothes," Felicity replied.

"We're leaving Monday, and we have, like, a billion things to buy," Claudia added.

"What's in *those* bags?" Mary-Kate asked, curious.

"Omigosh! Let me show you!" Felicity offered.

As Felicity and Claudia showed off the things they'd bought, Ashley felt a twinge of doubt.

Felicity had asked her to go to Spain, and Ashley had said no. She knew that had been the right decision. She really needed to work and make money this summer.

Still, watching Felicity and Claudia's excitement, Ashley couldn't help feeling as if her perfect summer was slowly but surely unraveling.

Felicity_girl invites Mary***Kate, AshleyO, and Claude18 to Instant Message!

Felicity_girl: 2 days to go and we
    still don't have enuf clothes.
Mary***Kate: Bring an empty suitcase &
    buy everything in Spain!!!
Claude18: Spanish clothes are way cool.
Felicity_girl: We'll look like Penelope
    Cruz.
AshleyO: Excellent!
Claude18: Who's up for tapas tonite?
AshleyO: Ta-what?
Claude18: Tiny foods they eat in Spain.
Felicity_girl: Not THAT tiny, I hope.
    I need food!!!!!
Mary***Kate: As long as it's food.
AshleyO: Count me in!

CHAPTER FIVE

Mary-Kate pulled the note out of her jeans and read it one more time.

Meet me behind Stable #45 at noon.
Very important!

Mary-Kate didn't recognize the handwriting. She had found the unsigned note in her backpack an hour ago. It was five minutes to noon now, and she was on her way to Stable #45. She wondered if the note had to do with Trevor. Maybe someone had found out about their relationship? Maybe someone who wanted him for herself? Maybe . . .

Stop it, Olsen! she chided herself, shaking her head. She had been thinking all kinds of silly, crazy thoughts ever since Aisha told her about Trevor's being voted "Most Eligible Guy" at the Silver Spurs Stables.

She hurried up the narrow trail, kicking up dust with each step. She only had half an hour for her lunch break, after which she had another two hours of mucking duty ahead of her.

She soon reached #45. It was away from the other stables, in a secluded location at the edge of the woods. In fact, it didn't even look as if it was in use.

Mary-Kate felt a shiver of nervousness. *Who wants to meet me way out here?* she wondered.

She approached the stable cautiously. A familiar figure appeared in the doorway. "Hungry?"

Mary-Kate laughed, happy and relieved. Trevor was standing there, holding a picnic basket in one hand. He grinned. "Surprised?"

Mary-Kate rushed up to him and gave him a big hug. "Um, yeah. A little. Actually, a lot!" she told him.

Trevor took her hand. "Come on. I picked out a killer spot for us. I disguised my handwriting so you wouldn't recognize it."

"You're way too smart."

Trevor led her to a pretty grass-covered clearing behind the stable. Wildflowers waved and bobbed in the breeze.

Trevor reached into the basket and pulled out a white blanket. He spread it on the ground. *"Voilà!"* he said. "See? High-school French does come in handy!"

Giggling, Mary-Kate sat down on the blanket. Trevor pulled off his boots and socks and sat down as well. He loved being barefoot. For as long as Mary-Kate had known him, he always took off his shoes whenever he had the opportunity.

"Let's see, what have we got?" Trevor began pulling

things out of the basket and spreading them out on the blanket. "Ham-and-cheese sandwiches. Well, ham-and-cheese sandwiches without ham. We were out. Potato chips. Soda. The soda might be kind of warm—I hope you don't mind."

"This is awesome. I can't believe you did all this for me!" Mary-Kate exclaimed, surveying the feast.

"Hey, only the best for my girlfriend," Trevor said.

Mary-Kate stared at him. *Did he just say the word* girlfriend? she asked herself. *Omigosh. Omigosh.*

But Trevor was just sitting there unwrapping a sandwich, whistling under his breath. He wasn't acting like someone who had just crossed the fine line from "just dating" to "boyfriend-girlfriend." Maybe she should get her hearing checked.

"So," Trevor said, handing her half a sandwich. "How's your day going?"

Mary-Kate told him about the tourists and other visitors she'd met while working on guided trail-ride duty. She also told him about her difficulties with Fred the horse.

Then, trying to sound supercasual, she said, "Guess what Aisha told me."

"What?" Trevor asked, munching a chip.

"She said that the girls here have named you 'Most Eligible Guy,'" Mary-Kate said.

Trevor burst into laughter. "No way! That's hilarious!"

"Way! They all think you look like Ben Affleck," Mary-Kate insisted.

"Ben Affleck, right," Trevor said, cracking up.

Then he stopped laughing and leaned forward, looking into Mary-Kate's eyes.

"Hey," he said softly. He seemed to sense that Aisha's gossip bothered her more than she was letting on. "I don't care what any of the girls here think about me—except you. As long as my girlfriend thinks I'm hot, that's all I care about."

Girlfriend! *He definitely said* girlfriend! Mary-Kate thought.

Trevor glanced around. They were completely alone. Then he wrapped his arms around Mary-Kate and kissed her. He tasted like potato chips.

Mary-Kate decided that sneaking around was a good thing after all.

A Sheryl Crow song blasted on the boom box and Ashley rocked to the beat. She, Mary-Kate, Felicity, and Claudia were dancing around a bonfire they had made. It was their good-bye party for Felicity and Claudia.

Ashley was as happy as she could be, considering that her two best buds were about to take off for a month. She and Mary-Kate had worked all day putting everything together: sandwiches, chips, sodas, and wood for the bonfire. They had even baked a special cake, shaped like Spain. Unfortunately, it looked more like Rhode Island.

"Let's jump in the waves!" Felicity said all of a sudden.

"Jump in the waves?" Ashley echoed, laughing. "Aren't you afraid that new sundress of yours is going to get ruined?"

"Who cares? I'll buy another one in Spain!" Felicity grabbed Ashley's hand and pulled her toward the water. Claudia and Mary-Kate followed, giggling.

Ashley rolled up the bottoms of her white Capri pants. She, Mary-Kate, Felicity, and Claudia counted to three, then jumped into a knee-high wave.

"Whoo-hoo!" Claudia screeched. "That was awesome!"

They continued jumping into the waves, then jumping out, screaming with laughter. Ashley loved this game, which they had been playing for years.

She liked the idea of growing up and going away to college. At the same time she *didn't* like the idea of leaving all *this* behind. Playing in the waves, partying under the stars, hanging out with her best friends in the whole world . . .

"This is freeeeezing!" Mary-Kate complained.

"Oh, stop being such a wimp!" Claudia chided her.

"Here comes a big one! Omigosh, run for it!" Ashley shouted.

The four girls turned and made a beeline for the

beach. They collapsed onto the sand, breathless and laughing, as the huge wave broke, rolled, and began to recede just inches away from their toes.

"Okay, so I have to say it. This is an awesome going-away party!" Felicity said, adjusting a strap on her soaked sundress.

"Totally," Claudia agreed.

"It almost makes me wish we weren't going away. We're going to miss an entire month of this," Felicity said, gesturing at the beach and the bonfire. "We're going to miss you guys."

Ashley felt a lump in her throat. "We're going to miss you guys, too."

"I know!" Mary-Kate said suddenly. "The four of us should plan to do something special when you guys get back from Spain. Something really, *really* special."

Ashley perked up. Leave it to her twin to turn a bleak moment into a brilliant idea. "Like what?" she asked eagerly.

"Like—I don't know. Like maybe . . . a camping trip? How about a camping trip?" Mary-Kate suggested.

"Yes, yes, yes," Felicity said, nodding.

"We'll have to ask our parents," Claudia pointed out. "I don't know about yours, but mine aren't going to let me go unless I agree to, like, ten thousand conditions."

"Same with ours," Ashley said. "But that's okay. It's worth it if we can do it."

Mary-Kate's eyes lit up. "Hey! I just thought of *the* place. Joshua Tree National Park."

"Oh, cool. I've always wanted to go there," Felicity said.

Claudia nodded. "Me, too. Camping in the desert! That's going to be so awesome."

The four girls started talking excitedly about when to go, what to pack, and what kind of food to bring. Mary-Kate mentioned trail mix. Claudia mentioned chocolate-chip cookies. Felicity mentioned nachos. She always needed nachos. "I'm sure they sell dehydrated nachos at the camping store," she said with a grin.

"Gross me out," Ashley said, laughing.

As they talked about the trip, Ashley's heart felt lighter than it had all night. Saying good-bye to Felicity and Claudia would be a little easier now, knowing that they had this special, private, just-the-girls adventure to look forward to at the end of the summer.

AshleyO invites Felicity_girl and Claude18 to Instant Message!

Felicity_girl: Can't talk. Packing.

Claude18: Me 2.

AshleyO: Okay, well, catch U later.

Felicity_girl: Def!

Claude18: Fel, don't forget bathing suits!

Felicity_girl: Duh.

Claude18: And running shoes.

Felicity_girl: Gotta stay in shape. Beach reading?

Claude18: Got it.

AshleyO: Okay, well, signing off.

Felicity_girl: Shd I bring my hair dryer or R U bringing yours?

AshleyO: Good night!

CHAPTER SIX

Ashley stood next to the microwave oven, waiting for her mug of coffee to heat up. She checked the contents of her breakfast tray. Toasted cinnamon-raisin bagel with extra butter. Check. Mango slices. Check. Vanilla yogurt with granola sprinkles. Check.

The timer went off; the coffee was ready. Ashley opened the microwave and retrieved her mug. Then she picked up the tray and headed for the stairs.

Breakfast in bed. She figured it would be a surefire cure for her bummed-out mood.

But why am I feeling like this? she wondered.

Duh! Cuz Felicity and Claudia are gone, she told herself.

Despite the fun time they'd had on the beach, despite the plans they'd made for a Joshua Tree camping trip, Ashley had woken up this morning in a funk. Mary-Kate was still asleep, so Ashley couldn't commiserate with her.

Ashley reached the hallway and was just about to go upstairs when she noticed something out of the corner of her eye—a small pile of envelopes on the hall table.

Must be from yesterday, she thought. She had been so busy getting ready for the party that she hadn't had time to check the mail.

Setting the tray down on the table, Ashley sifted through the envelopes. One of them was addressed to her, in dark purple ink on silver-flecked paper.

Cool stationery, Ashley thought. There was no return address. She wondered who the letter was from.

She put the envelope on her breakfast tray and carried the whole thing up to her room. Once there she set the tray on her bed and ripped open the envelope.

There was a letter inside, in unfamiliar-looking handwriting.

Dear Ashley,
You don't know me—yet! But I just found out that I'm going to be your college roommate at Lawton this fall. I live in Lincoln, Nebraska. Below is my contact info. Feel free to write or call whenever you want!

The letter was signed: *Zoe Hanover.* Below her name was an address, phone number, and e-mail address.

Suddenly Ashley forgot about her bad mood. Here was a blast of good news, a reminder of her exciting new future: a note from her college roommate!

She took a big bite of her cinnamon-raisin bagel, then picked up her cordless phone. What time zone was Nebraska in anyway? It couldn't be *that* early, since it was already ten in California, Ashley thought.

She punched in Zoe's number. After a few rings a girl's voice answered. "Hello?"

"Hi, this is Ashley Olsen. Is Zoe there?"

"This is Zoe. Hey! It's nice to meet you. On the phone, that is."

"It's nice to meet you, too," Ashley told her. "I just got your letter. Cool stationery."

"Thanks. What time is it there?"

"Ten in the morning. Am I calling too early?"

"Oh, no way. It's noon here, and I've been up since six. I ran for, like, two hours and then did laps in our pool."

"Oh, wow."

Zoe is obviously a superathlete, Ashley thought. She decided not to mention the fact that she herself had just gotten up and was now drowning her sorrows in a buttered bagel and coffee.

The two of them spent the next half hour exchanging details about their lives. Ashley told Zoe all about her excellent summer job at the Caribe Beach Club. Zoe told her about *her* summer job working as a camp counselor. Ashley told Zoe about Mary-Kate. Zoe told Ashley all about *her* sibs: two older brothers and a baby sister.

After a while Ashley decided that she really liked Zoe. She seemed supersweet and easy to talk to. Ashley was glad they'd been matched up by the college to be roommates.

"So, are you psyched about starting college?" Ashley asked Zoe.

"Oh, yeah! Definitely! I'm psyched about our dorm, too. It's supposed to be really cool."

"I guess we should coordinate on décor for our room," Ashley said. "I was thinking of buying some sheets and stuff at the mall this week."

"Yeah! I was thinking of all black," Zoe said.

Ashley did a mental double take. "All . . . *black*?" she repeated.

"Uh-huh. You know. Black sheets, black bed-spreads, black curtains, black walls," Zoe said.

"Black . . . walls," Ashley said, confused. "Are you sure about this? I mean, I love black as much as the next person. I have more little black dresses than any-one I know. But don't we want some, you know, *color* in our room?"

But Zoe didn't seem to hear her. "Come to think of it, I'm not sure if the college'll let us paint the walls black. Maybe it's against the rules, or whatever. In that case we could just buy extra black sheets and use them to cover the walls."

As Zoe continued babbling about the black décor, Ashley found herself wondering: Who *was* this weird person who was so obsessed with the color black?

More important, was it too early to request a roommate switch?

"We're here," Trevor announced.

It was Sunday afternoon. Trevor had called Mary-Kate out of the blue and asked her to come for a drive with him.

Trevor stopped his Jeep on the edge of a cliff. Below them was a long, secluded stretch of beach.

"This is . . . *awesome*," Mary-Kate said slowly. "Where are we? I've never seen this beach before."

"I drove by it last week and wanted to check it out. Come on."

Trevor jumped out of the car, then came over to her side to open the door for her. He took her hand in his and led her over a gently sloping trail that meandered down the side of the cliff.

What a cool beach! Mary-Kate thought.

Walking past wildflowers and sea grasses, listening to the gulls and other birds whistling and shrieking in the air, Mary-Kate felt happy, carefree, light. She loved being here. And she loved being with Trevor.

She stared at Trevor's broad shoulders, at his tousled brown hair, as he picked his way down the hill. She loved . . . *him*. The truth came to her as easily as breath. Her heart swelled with the rightness of it.

Trevor turned and smiled at her. "Almost there."

"Okay."

Trevor squeezed her hand and led her to a stretch of pristine sand. Sandpipers had left rows of tiny footprints.

The two of them sat down on the sand. Travis wrapped an arm around her shoulders and planted a kiss on her cheek. Then he started to tickle her. It was their old game from before. She tickled him back, screeching and laughing.

"Look!" Travis stopped tickling her and pointed. "A dolphin!"

"Where?"

"There!"

Mary-Kate stared out at the water. Suddenly a large, dark gray shape rose out of a wave. It made a quick, graceful arc in the air, then disappeared.

"Are you sure it's a dolphin? Maybe it's a seal or a walrus."

"Of course it's a dolphin, you freak. It jumped out of the water!"

"It also kinda looked like a shark."

"You are hopeless!" Trevor teased her.

Mary-Kate grinned. Then she gazed out at the ocean. "This is so cool," she said. "Thanks for bringing me here."

"Everything we do together is cool," Trevor told her, his voice suddenly serious.

Mary-Kate turned to look at him. He was smiling

at her, and his brown eyes seemed to be trying to tell her . . . *something.*

Was it *I love you*? she wondered. Because she knew now, in this special, beautiful place, that *she* loved *him.*

Maybe I should say it first, she thought.

Taking a deep breath, summoning up her courage, she opened her mouth to speak.

Just then Trevor drew away from her ever so slightly and said, "So have you been thinking about college?"

Mary-Kate was taken aback. College had been the last thing on her mind. "What?"

"You know, *college.* You're going to be going away this fall."

Just like that, Mary-Kate felt the romantic mood collapse. The spell was broken. She had been ready to tell him the three most important words she'd ever said to anyone. And here he was, bringing up the subject of college.

She was going to be heading east to New York with Ashley. And Trevor was going to be staying out west, to attend the Pacific School of Design, an art college in L.A.

Is he trying to tell me something? she wondered.

"Sorry, did I interrupt you? You looked like you were about to say something," Trevor said.

Mary-Kate shook her head. "No," she replied, trying to keep her voice from catching in her throat. "I wasn't going to say anything."

AshleyO invites Felicity_girl, Claude18, and Mary★★★Kate to Instant Message!

AshleyO: Hey, U jet-setters! How R U?

Felicity_girl: Jet-laggers is more like it.

Claude18: Serious baggy eyes.

AshleyO: Tea bags, remember? What does Barcelona look like?

Felicity_girl: Lots of old buildings.

Claude18: Really old.

Felicity_girl: Cute guys.

Claude18: REALLY cute guys.

AshleyO: We miss U!

Felicity_girl: We miss U 2!

Claude18: Hey MK?? How R U? How's Trevor?

Mary★★★Kate: Don't ask.

Felicity_girl: What? Details, please.

Mary★★★Kate: Don't ask.

Claude18: Uh-oh.

CHAPTER SEVEN

What kind of smoothies do you have? Excuse me, miss? *Miss?*"

Ashley glanced up. A woman with a huge purple hat was frowning at her.

"Oh, I'm so sorry! We have peach, strawberry, blueberry, raspberry, and a superspecial combo," Ashley rattled off.

"I'll take the blueberry," the woman said. "My, the service is slow around here!"

"I'm sorry!" Ashley apologized.

As Ashley threw blueberries into the blender, she chided herself: *Get it together, Olsen!* She had been really spacey today. Oh, well. It was Monday, which was a spacey day, anyway.

And Felicity and Claudia were in Spain.

As Ashley turned on the blender, she pictured Felicity and Claudia at some fab restaurant. She tried to imagine what they were wearing. *Matching sundresses, probably, with suede bolero jackets, thigh-high leather boots, and killer shades.*

Ashley reminded herself that Felicity had asked her first, and she had said no. Ashley was glad she'd stayed behind to make money and spend some time with Mary-Kate. She had never been away from her sister for an entire month. That would have been weird.

Still, Ashley's planned summer of fun was not exactly—well—fun. She liked her job at the beach club. But her best buds were on the other side of the Atlantic Ocean. And even Mary-Kate was scarce. She was spending most of her free time with Trevor these days, though she'd never really explained her "don't ask" comment from the other day. All Mary-Kate had said when Ashley asked her about it later was that she and Trevor were totally focused on spending the summer together. *I've got to sit her down and find out what's going on,* Ashley thought.

"Here you go." Ashley handed the blueberry smoothie to the woman with the purple hat. The woman harrumphed, handed her some money, and left.

A girl in a green bathing suit marched up to the counter. "That woman needs an attitude adjustment," she remarked. "So. What exactly is a smoothie anyway?"

Ashley stared at her in astonishment. "You don't know what a smoothie is?"

The girl shook her head. She had short, sun-streaked red hair, freckles, and hazel eyes. "Nah. As far as I'm concerned, the four major food groups consist of popcorn, pizza, soda, and ice cream. Anything else is not worth eating."

"Wow, you're pretty extreme," Ashley said. "I don't think you'd be into smoothies, then. Although I guess I shouldn't be saying that. I mean, you're a potential customer. I'm supposed to be talking you *into* buying a smoothie."

"Actually, I'm not a customer. I'm Kim. The new girl."

Ashley frowned. "The . . . what?"

"I'm the new replacement for the towel girl, who, like, took off for Portugal or Spain or whatever," Kim explained.

"Oh!" Ashley introduced herself to Kim. "Did Nico hire you?" she asked.

"You mean the guy with the lethal-weapon toenails? Yeah. I don't think he liked me very much, but I could tell he was kind of desperate to hire someone ASAP," Kim said, cracking her knuckles. "Did you check out that flying, talking *freak* he's got for a pet? Before the summer's over, I'm planning on teaching it some swear words."

Ashley cracked up. Kim was kind of intense, but in a good way.

"I'm glad you're going to be working here," Ashley told her. "Felicity and Claudia—they're the girls who took off for Spain—are my best friends. I was kind of bummed when they decided to go on this trip. I mean, it was, like, who am I going to get manicures and have slumber parties with?"

Kim rolled her eyes at her. "Manicures? Slumber parties? Wow, you sure do hang out with a different crowd," she remarked.

"Excuse me?" Ashley said, taken aback.

Kim held up a hand. "Sorry, that came out wrong. Listen, I may not be into manicures, and I kind of stopped the slumber party thing when I was, like, nine. But I don't know anyone here. And you're missing your buds. So why don't we hang out?"

"Sure," Ashley said. Kim wasn't exactly Ms. Tactful, but she did seem cool. "That would be fun."

"Like, are you doing anything tonight? You want to check out that new movie at the mall?"

"The Jude Law movie?" Ashley said eagerly.

"Jude Law? No way. I'm talking about the new sci-fi, action-adventure movie about rogue 'bots taking over the White House," Kim replied.

"Oh."

"My treat. We can pig out on artificially flavored popcorn," Kim said, slapping Ashley on the arm. "Come on, you look as if you need some serious cheering up."

Ashley smiled. Kim was right. "Okay, rogue 'bots it is," she said.

• • •

On Saturday night Mary-Kate met Trevor at the Café Iguana.

"What are you going to have?" she asked him as they checked out the handwritten menus.

"Uh, I don't know. Maybe an extra-large decaf soy chai latte with a shot of, uh, lingonberry syrup," Trevor said, grinning.

Mary-Kate knew he was joking. He wouldn't know what a soy chai latte was if someone poured it over his head.

"I'm having carrot cake," Mary-Kate decided.

"Cool. Can I have some of it?"

"Get your own," Mary-Kate teased him.

The two of them exchanged details about their day. Trevor told her a long, gory story about helping his dad clean the basement and all the old, embarrassing stuff they'd found down there. Mary-Kate updated him about Felicity and Claudia's adventures in Spain.

"You and Ashley must be bummed, huh?" Trevor said, squeezing her hand. "I mean, that you don't have them to hang out with."

He understands! See? This isn't bad, she reassured herself. *We're perfect together.* "Big-time." Mary-Kate nodded. "Especially Ashley. First she lost her job. And now she's lost two of her best buds—for a month anyway. This summer isn't going exactly the way she planned."

The waiter came by and took their orders. Just then

Mary-Kate noticed a couple of girls entering the café.

Then Mary-Kate recognized the girls. *Oh, no!* Gasping, she yanked her hand away from Trevor.

"What? *What?*" Trevor asked her. "Did I suddenly develop bad breath or something?" he joked.

"Aisha and Danielle just walked in!" Mary-Kate whispered fiercely. "They're coming over here!"

"Oh, great," Trevor muttered.

"Hey," Aisha called out, coming up to Mary-Kate and Trevor. "Is this a peace summit?"

"Hi, Trevor," Danielle said, sidling up to him. "How's it going?"

"We, uh, decided we should be friends, since we work together," Mary-Kate improvised. *Does Danielle have to stand so close to Trevor?* she wondered irritably.

Trevor jumped to his feet, trying to avoid Danielle. "I'm, uh, gonna check out the tunes. Excuse me."

"Oh, me, too! I'll go with you," Danielle offered.

Trevor mouthed the words *I'm sorry!* to Mary-Kate before taking off for the jukebox, followed by a clingy Danielle.

Mary-Kate tried not to look as annoyed as she felt. *Why—why?—did Aisha and Danielle have to show up at the café?* she wondered.

"That girl doesn't know the meaning of the word *subtle*," Aisha said, rolling her eyes. "Poor Trevor! Look at his expression. 'Get me out of here!'" she said, mimicking his voice.

Mary-Kate laughed. "You're right. He does look pretty unhappy."

Aisha wrapped an arm around Mary-Kate's shoulders. "Listen," she said in a low voice, "I need your help."

"Sure," Mary-Kate replied, surprised. "What's up?"

"This is top secret, okay?" Aisha said.

Mary-Kate nodded. "Okay."

"See, I like this guy," Aisha went on. "A guy at the stables. And I need your help snagging him."

"Oh!" Mary-Kate said. "No problem. Who is it?"

"It's—"

"We're back!" Danielle broke in. She and Trevor were standing there. "We checked out the dessert tray, too, but it was way too carby and sugary."

"Carby?" Trevor repeated, looking confused.

"I'm more in the mood for a smoothie, anyway," Aisha said. "Come on, Danielle, let's go down the street."

"Sure! Bye, Trev! Bye, Mary-Kate."

Before Mary-Kate could say anything, the two girls took off.

"Miss me?" Trevor asked her after they'd gone.

"Definitely," Mary-Kate said. "That Danielle girl's kinda getting on my nerves."

"Ditto!"

The waiter brought their drinks and desserts. As she and Trevor dug in, Mary-Kate wondered, *Who could Aisha's secret crush be?*

AshleyO invites Felicity_girl and Claude18 to Instant Message!

Felicity_girl and Claude18 are not available.

CHAPTER EIGHT

I s this horse dangerous?"

"What's that nasty smell?"

"I want my mommy!"

Mary-Kate sighed. A bunch of workers had called in sick at the stables. The place was seriously under-staffed. So she had been working the guided trail rides all morning, two and three horses at a time.

Mary-Kate tried to reassure the various kids. No, the horse wasn't dangerous. It was a nice, horsey, farm smell, not a nasty smell. And the ride would be over in just five minutes.

Mary-Kate urged the horses ahead. She wanted the ride to be over as much as the kids did. She wanted to take a break and find Aisha so they could resume their conversation from Saturday night.

Who could Aisha's secret crush be? Mary-Kate wondered a second time that morning. *And what does she want* moi *to do about it?*

Finally the ride was over. Mary-Kate helped the little kids off their horses and reunited them with their parents. Then she grabbed a soda from the vending machine and went off in search of Aisha.

She found her washing out a feed bucket. "Hey!" Mary-Kate said, waving.

Aisha turned, spotted Mary-Kate, and waved back. "Hey, girlfriend!" she called out. "Where've you been hiding all morning?"

"Trail rides. Cranky kids. Need I say more?"

Aisha laughed and shook her head. "Nah. Boss Lady's been supercranky, too. I think this is one of those bad-Monday situations. Let's pray for this day to be over, fast."

Mary-Kate put her hands on her hips. "Okay, enough about work. We were in the middle of a *very* interesting conversation on Saturday night," she reminded Aisha, wiggling her eyebrows.

"Oh, yeah." Aisha blushed. "*That*. Listen, I need some advice from you." She glanced around, then lowered her voice. "What would you do if you really, really liked a guy but you weren't sure he liked you?"

Mary-Kate was taken aback by Aisha's question. "Well, it depends," she said slowly. "Are you friends?"

"Sort of. Not really. I mean, we know each other and everything, but we haven't hung out or anything," Aisha replied.

"Well, that might be a start," Mary-Kate advised her. "The best way to go from zero to romance is to become friends first. Not that I would *know*," she added quickly. "After all, I'm totally unattached!"

Mary-Kate didn't like lying to Aisha. But she and Trevor were determined to keep their relationship under wraps. It felt more special that way. Besides, Mary-Kate didn't want to become part of the Silver Spurs gossip mill.

"Yeah, I see your point," Aisha agreed. "The thing is, I don't think I have a chance with him. He's way too cool. He's way too cute. He's way too . . . *everything.*"

"Don't sell yourself short," Mary-Kate insisted. "This guy may be supercool and cute. But you're supercool and cute, too. You have to approach these situations with confidence!" She added again, "Not that I would know, since I'm totally unattached." She laughed nervously.

Aisha leaned forward and squeezed Mary-Kate's arm. "I'm not sure I can do this alone. And Danielle, well . . . she wouldn't be the best help. Can you be my romance coach, or whatever, and help me get this guy?"

"Uh, sure," Mary-Kate said. "I'm not sure how good a romance coach I'm going to be, since I'm totally unattached. But, sure. Whatever I can do to help."

"Great!" Aisha beamed.

"But first you're going to have to tell me who he is," Mary-Kate told Aisha.

Aisha blushed again. "You're never going to guess. Or maybe you will, since every other girl here is after him. It's Trevor Reynolds!" she announced.

Mary-Kate almost choked on her soda.

This isn't happening, she thought.

Ashley leaned back in her beach chair and slathered some sunscreen onto her arms. She was taking a break from work. She really needed to chill out, breathe some salty ocean air, and try to figure out how to save what was left of her summer.

She hadn't heard from Felicity and Claudia in a while. And every time she tried to IM them, they seemed to be unavailable. Sure, there was a big time difference, like nine hours or so, but were they having so much fun that they couldn't be bothered to talk to her? Or even send a postcard? Or had they forgotten about her altogether?

Ashley sighed. She knew she was overreacting. Still, without Felicity and Claudia, and with Mary-Kate hanging out with Trevor all the time, she was *definitely* not having a good summer.

Ashley's cell phone rang. She checked out the number on her Caller ID, but it was an unfamiliar area code.

"Hello?"

"Hey, Ashley? It's Zoe."

It was Ashley's new roommate. "Oh, hey, Zoe,"

Ashley said. "How's it going? I'm at work right now."

"Oh, am I bothering you?"

"No, it's okay. I'm on a break."

Ashley had been working up to talking to Zoe about the all-black décor. Maybe this was a good time.

"Listen, Zoe, I've been thinking about our room—" Ashley began.

"Oh, yeah," Zoe interrupted. "Listen, I've been rethinking that, too. And I think the all-black thing is lame."

"You do?" Ashley said, surprised.

"Yeah. So last year. I think we should go for, like, all faux leopard skin," Zoe suggested.

Ashley did a mental double take. "Faux . . . leopard?" she repeated.

"It's all over the runways. Faux leopard is in! I read about it in *Vogue*."

"You did?"

"And listen! I've been researching the New York City club scene. Most of them don't even open until midnight, did you know that? I figured we could try a different one every night."

A different club every night? Ashley got sleepy just thinking about it. What kind of wild girl *was* Zoe anyway?

"Well, it was great talking to you," Zoe said. "I've gotta go. I have an appointment for a healing Dead Sea mud treatment."

Wow, Nebraska must be a hipper place than I thought, Ashley mused. "Okay. Talk to you later."

"Think leopard!"

"Okay."

Zoe hung up. Ashley stared at the phone. First the all-black décor. Now faux leopard and all-night clubbing.

The more she got to know Zoe, the more she was convinced: She and Zoe were total opposites!

Felicity_girl invites AshleyO to Instant Message!

AshleyO: Hey! Hi!

Felicity_girl: Hola!

AshleyO: Howz it going over there?

Felicity_girl: Mui excellente!
Everything is great!

AshleyO: Great!

Felicity_girl: Howz the Beach Club?

AshleyO: Well, actually, it's not the
same without—

Felicity_girl: Ash? Dad just got back,
and we're grabbing dinner. Did U
know that they eat at, like, 11 PM
over here? Wild! I'll talk to U
later, K? Adios!

CHAPTER NINE

Listen, Aisha, I happen to know that Trevor isn't
available.

Listen, Aisha, Trevor and I are kind of . . . dating.

Listen, Aisha, Trevor already has a girlfriend. Me!

Listen, Aisha, keep your hands off him—or else!

Mary-Kate paced around the barn, mentally
rehearsing what, exactly, she was going to say to Aisha.
She had been stewing about it ever since Aisha
dropped her bombshell.

Her first impulse had been to tell Trevor. But
Ashley had talked her out of it.

"That would be really embarrassing for Aisha,"
Ashley had told her after Mary-Kate spilled the whole
story. "You need to talk to *her*, not him. You need to
tell her the truth about your relationship with Trevor."

That seemed like good advice, Mary-Kate thought.

The problem was, she wasn't sure how Aisha would
react. What if she got really upset? Or what if she got
downright mad? Aisha wasn't the sort of person to
hold anything back.

"Yo, Mary-Kate!"

Mary-Kate turned around. Aisha sauntered into the barn, carrying a bucket of feed.

"Hey, Aisha," Mary-Kate said, forcing herself to smile. Inside, she thought, *Uh-oh, here we go.*

Aisha walked up to her and set the bucket down. "So! Have you figured out a love strategy for me yet?" she asked eagerly.

"A love strategy?" Mary-Kate repeated. "Well, not exactly. Listen, Aisha, there's something I have to tell you."

Aisha grinned. "Sure. What's up?"

"It's about Trevor . . ." Mary-Kate began.

"You mean, the man of my dreams," Aisha said with a giggle.

Aisha was making it really hard for her to spill her guts. Mary-Kate took a deep breath, fortifying herself. "Well, that's what I want to talk to you about. See, I happen to know that Trevor is . . ." Mary-Kate paused.

Aisha smiled at her. "Trevor is what?"

"What I mean is, Trevor isn't exactly . . ."

"Yeah? I'm all ears."

"What I mean is, Trevor and . . . well, that is, Trevor and I . . ." Mary-Kate blushed.

Just then Aisha burst out laughing.

Mary-Kate stared at her. "What is so *funny*?" she demanded.

"You should've seen the look on your face!" Aisha exclaimed. She was laughing so hard that tears were streaming down her cheeks.

Mary-Kate put her hands on her hips. "*What* look on my face?"

"The look on your face when I told you that I wanted you to help me snag your boyfriend!" Aisha replied.

"*What?*" Mary-Kate cried out. "You knew all along?"

Aisha nodded, doubling over with laughter.

Mary-Kate wasn't sure whether to be relieved or angry. Aisha had deliberately set her up!

"Listen, I'm sorry," Aisha said, wiping tears from her face. "I figured out weeks ago that you and Trevor were in *L-O-V-E*. Major sparks fly between you two every time you're together. And whenever you see Danielle, you look like you could pound her into the ground! But you were so totally secretive about it. I just wanted you to admit it."

Mary-Kate smiled. So *that's* what Aisha had been up to. "You could have just asked me," she pointed out.

"Yeah, I guess. But this way was more fun!" Aisha giggled.

Mary-Kate laughed, too. "*Fun?* It was more like torture!"

Aisha reached over and gave Mary-Kate a hug.

"Don't worry, okay? I'll get the word out about the two of you so everyone—read, *Danielle*—will know that Trevor is off-limits!"

"Thanks," Mary-Kate said.

"So how long have you two been in *L-O-V-E*, anyway?" Aisha asked her.

Mary-Kate frowned. "Well . . . that is . . . we haven't exactly said the *L-O-V-E* thing to each other yet," she admitted.

Aisha slapped her on the back. "Girl! You'd better get busy and say something, because it's totally obvious that you two are head over heels."

"Really?" Mary-Kate asked happily.

"Really!" Aisha replied. "Now, let's think. Atmosphere is everything—you know that, right? You need to take your man somewhere romantic."

"Like where?"

"Like where? Like—hey, how about the carnival? Now *that's* romantic," Aisha suggested.

Mary-Kate made a face. She'd tried to confess her feelings to Trevor in the Tunnel of Love at the amusement park during Senior Cut Day. What she'd ended up doing was dropping her camera into the machinery and breaking the whole ride. "Going to freak shows and getting cotton candy stuck all over your face is romantic?"

Aisha sighed dramatically. "No, no, no. Going on scary rides together is romantic. Hey, I know! Why don't you make your love announcement at the top of the Ferris wheel?"

"The Ferris wheel," Mary-Kate said slowly. She liked the idea. "Yes!"

"Great! Go for it! And now you still need to help me with a love strategy," Aisha told her.

"I thought you said that was a joke," Mary-Kate said, confused.

Aisha shook her head. "The part about Trevor was a joke. But I really do like a guy. His name is Grant."

"The riding instructor?" Mary-Kate asked her. Aisha nodded. "I don't know him, but he's definitely cute!"

"Definitely and absolutely," Aisha agreed. "So are you going to help me, or what?"

"Definitely and absolutely," Mary-Kate replied.

"Hey," Aisha said suddenly. "Aren't you going to New York City for college? Is Trevor going with you?"

Mary-Kate frowned. "Uh, well, no. Not exactly."

"Is that going to be a problem?" Aisha asked her.

"I'm not sure," Mary-Kate replied.

Mary-Kate reached into her jeans pocket and felt the folded-up piece of paper she had in there. It was the Web site address for Trevor's college.

She hadn't told a soul, not even Ashley. But she had been meaning to download an application for the school. She would get around to it tonight. It couldn't hurt just to take a look.

• • •

"Step right up! Tickets, please."

It was Saturday night. The Ferris-wheel operator took two tickets from Mary-Kate as she stepped onto the platform. She glanced over her shoulder at Trevor, who was holding a large stuffed bear. Or maybe it was a squirrel. Or a walrus. Whatever it was, it was kind of ugly. But Mary-Kate wasn't going to complain. Trevor had won it for her at one of the ball-toss games, and he was really proud of it.

"Are you coming?" Mary-Kate asked him, extending a hand.

He took her hand and stepped onto the platform. He planted a kiss on her nose. "Sure. I hope Fuzzy here doesn't need a ticket, too!" he joked, indicating the stuffed animal.

Mary-Kate smiled. "I don't know. He's pretty big."

The two of them got into a carriage. It swung back and forth gently as they settled into their seat.

"Here we go," Trevor said, draping an arm around Mary-Kate's shoulders. He put Fuzzy on her lap.

The Ferris wheel started up, then stopped as more people got on. Mary-Kate nestled her head on Trevor's shoulder as the Ferris wheel continued turning. She felt giddy and nervous with anticipation, thinking about what would happen at the top. She was finally going to tell him how she really felt about him. And if all went as planned, he would say the same three wonderful, amazing words back to her.

I love you, Trevor.

I love you, Mary-Kate.

Mary-Kate smiled.

"What?" Trevor asked her.

"Hmm?"

"What are you smiling about?"

"Oh, nothing. I mean, I was just thinking about how much fun I'm having," Mary-Kate said, improvising.

Trevor smiled and kissed her. His lips tasted like cotton candy. "Me, too," he said.

Mary-Kate's heart skipped a beat. Everything Trevor did and said made her feel happy and in love.

She couldn't wait to tell him. They were almost at the top now. Down below was the carnival, with its bright lights, whirring rides, and cheerful carousel music. Up above was the night sky, glittering with stars.

This is it, Mary-Kate thought excitedly. *This is our big moment—*

"By the way," Trevor said suddenly. "I've been thinking about college some more."

"You've been ... what?" Mary-Kate asked, startled.

Trevor turned his face slightly, and she couldn't read his expression. "You know, college. I mean, do you want us to see other people while we're at college, or what?" he asked slowly.

Mary-Kate felt the color draining out of her face.

What was Trevor talking about? And why was he bringing this up *now*, of all times?

She had finally downloaded an application for his college and started to fill it out. Then she'd stopped. Then she'd started again. It was sitting in her desk drawer right now. But she wasn't ready to tell him about that yet.

Right now she didn't even know what to say in response to his question. "Why, do you?" she finally managed.

"That's not what I said. What I said was, what do *you* want? Or were you just planning on breaking up with me at the end of the summer?" Trevor asked, sounding upset.

"How can you say that?" Mary-Kate demanded. "I just figured that when we went away to college . . ."

"That what? We would just kind of keep going the way we were? How can we do that when we're going to be, like, three thousand miles away from each other?"

"I don't know."

They were at the top of the Ferris wheel now. Mary-Kate was on the verge of crying.

Instead of saying *I love you* to each other, they were having their very first argument.

This was *not* the way it was supposed to happen.

AshleyO invites Felicity_girl, Mary★★★Kate, and Claude18 to Instant Message!

AshleyO: Hey!

Felicity_girl: Hola!

Claudia18: Hola!

AshleyO: How R U guys? Howz Spain?

Felicity_girl: Bueno!

AshleyO: Great. Hey, I was thinking we
    should start planning 4 Joshua Tree.

Felicity_girl: Joshua who?

Mary★★★Kate: U have boyz on the brain.
    Joshua TREE, as in our camping trip!

Claude18: Oh, yeah.

Felicity_girl: Sure, let's plan!

Claude18: Fel!!!!

AshleyO: Hello?

Mary★★★Kate: Hello?

Felicity_girl: Gotta go. ASHTON
    KUTCHER just walked into the
    restaurant!!!!!!!!!!!!!!!!!!!!!!!!!!!

CHAPTER TEN

Astrawberry smoothie, please. Large."

Ashley set a bowl of fresh berries down on the counter and glanced at her customer. He was tall, blond, and supercute.

But today tall, blond, and supercute did nothing for her. She was having a blue day.

In fact, she was having a blue *week*. Month. Summer. Ashley really, really missed Felicity and Claudia.

She also missed *talking* to them. Their IMs lately had been totally out of sync. Either they were unavailable or too busy to chat for very long. *Sorry we haven't written! So crazy-busy! No sleep last night, too many parties! Will write more soon! Adiós!*

At least Kim's been around, Ashley thought. Even though she and Kim had almost nothing in common, they'd been having a lot of fun hanging out together. Kim was a good listener, and she gave smart, savvy advice. Ashley had found herself talking to Kim more and more about everything that was going on in her life: Felicity and Claudia's trip, their upcoming visit to Joshua Tree National Park, Mary-Kate and Trevor's romance, college.

Ashley sighed. Senior Summer wasn't turning out at all the way she'd expected. Sure, she had a fun job. But her best buds were incommunicado, her sister was involved in a hot and heavy romance, and college . . . well, college was coming up all too fast. With a weird roommate who had an all-leopard décor planned for their dorm room.

Ashley finished making the strawberry smoothie for Mr. Tall, Blond, and Supercute and handed it to him. "Here you go."

"Thanks," he said, flashing her two rows of perfect white teeth. Ashley barely noticed.

Just then she realized she was out of paper cups. She turned around, stood up on tiptoe, and began rummaging through the cupboard at the back of the stand.

It was total chaos in there. A stack of cups fell on her head, then scattered all over the floor.

"Oh, great," Ashley muttered.

"Can we get some smoothies?" a voice called out.

"Just a sec—"

"We're kind of in a hurry."

"Just a *second*," Ashley said impatiently. She bent down to pick up the cups.

"Listen, smoothie-girl. Don't you know who we are?"

Ashley whirled around. How *dare* anyone call her *smoothie-girl*?

There were two very tan girls standing on the other side of the counter. They were dressed in matching black sun hats, sleek black tankinis, and oversized shades. Their faces were obscured by the hats and sunglasses, but there was something familiar-looking about them. Were they actresses? Rock stars? Or just obnoxious poseurs?

"Can I help you?" Ashley snapped.

"Sure, smoothie-girl. You got any nachos around here?" the second girl said with a grin.

The two girls burst into laughter. What's going on here? Ashley wondered, irritated. *Nachos? Can't they see the sign says* "Smoothies"?

And then it dawned on Ashley. These two weren't famous superstars.

They were . . .

"You guys!" Ashley shouted.

The first one took her shades off. Then the second one did, too.

"Felicity!" Ashley screamed. "Claudia!"

"Ash!" Felicity and Claudia screamed.

Ashley ran out from behind the counter and wrapped her arms around her friends in a massive hug. The girls hugged her, too.

"We're home!" Felicity announced. "We got in on the red-eye. Or is it the opposite of the red-eye?"

"I don't know," Claudia said, giggling.

Ashley noticed that Felicity and Claudia smelled identical, like expensive sunscreen. They also had the same color tans and the same perfect manicures. They looked really . . . stunning, like models out of a fashion magazine.

"Why didn't you *tell* me you were coming home today?" Ashley demanded.

"We wanted to surprise you," Felicity replied, tucking her shades into her black linen beach bag. "Dad had to cut his trip a few days short. So—are you surprised, *chica*?"

"Definitely," Ashley said happily. "So how was the trip? How was Spain? Tell me everything!"

"Spain was *muy excelente*," Felicity said. "The cafés were fabulous. The clubs were even more fabulous."

"Tell her about the restaurants!" Claudia reminded Felicity.

"Oh, the restaurants!" Felicity gushed. "Claudia and I practically lived on paella the whole time we were there."

"Pie-what?" Ashley said, confused.

"Paella," Claudia explained, pronouncing it like *pie-a-ya*. "It's a fabulous rice dish with seafood and saffron in it."

"Cool." Ashley smiled.

"Oh, and last week we went to Bilbao," Felicity went on.

"Bill-who?" Ashley said.

"Bilbao. It's an incredible art museum in the Basque region of Spain," Felicity explained. "It's Gehry's creation."

Picking up on Ashley's frown, Felicity added, "You know, Frank Gehry. The architect. He just did the L.A. Philharmonic."

"Oh, sure," Ashley said, nodding without really understanding.

Felicity and Claudia continued talking about things and places Ashley had never heard of: Costa del Sol, Ibiza, Valencia, Majorca. Ashley smiled and listened, trying to keep up.

"Hey, dude, you want to grab some lunch?"

Ashley turned around. Kim was standing there. She was dressed in a green tank suit with a baggy white T-shirt over it that read: SOLAR POWER.

"Oh, hey!" Ashley called out. For some reason she was relieved that Kim had arrived.

Kim glanced at Felicity and Claudia. Her eyes widened slightly. "Hey," she said.

"*Hola!*" Felicity said. Claudia gave Kim a little wave.

Kim looked at Ashley as if to say, *What planet are these people from?* Ashley smiled weakly and said, "Kim, these are the friends I told you about, Felicity and Claudia. Guys, this is Kim. She started working here after you left for Spain."

"Oh! *Sí!* It's a pleasure," Felicity said, extending one of her perfectly manicured hands.

"Sure," Kim said, shaking her hand. "So you two just got back?"

"Just," Claudia replied. "Our bodies are still in a different time zone, though."

"You can say that again! *My* body thinks it's time for paella," Felicity said, chuckling.

"Pie-what?" Kim whispered to Ashley.

"Tell you later," Ashley whispered back.

Kim shrugged. "So," she said to Felicity and Claudia. "Ash here's been telling me all about your big camping trip."

"Our big camping trip?" Felicity repeated, looking blank for a moment. "Oh, yeah. Joshua Tree, right?"

"Sleeping in tents will be a big change after our four-star hotel in Barcelona." Claudia giggled. "Won't it, Fel?"

"Sí!"

The two girls cracked up.

"Okay, well, Kim and I are going to grab some lunch," Ashley said. "Do you two want to come?"

"Love to, but we have to decompress," Felicity replied. "Catch you later?"

Decompress? Ashley shrugged. "Sure. Later."

"Hasta la vista!" Claudia called out, waving.

Ashley waved back.

Felicity and Claudia had certainly . . . changed.

Ashley wished Mary-Kate was around just then. She needed to talk to someone who would understand. *Someone who can help me understand how I feel right now,* she thought.

Did they forget about the camping trip? Did they forget how they all usually talked?

Did they forget me?

AshleyO invites Mary★★★Kate to Instant Message!

AshleyO: Hey, U there?

Mary★★★Kate: Kinda jammed with riders right now. What's up?

AshleyO: Fel and Claude are back.

Mary★★★Kate: No kidding? Wow! That's great!

AshleyO: Yeah. They look gr8, like movie stars!

Mary★★★Kate: I can't wait 2 see them.

AshleyO: Can we get 2gether 2night?

Mary★★★Kate: Can't. Got plans.

AshleyO: With Trevor :-X

Mary★★★Kate: Well, sorta. About Trevor, you cd say.

AshleyO: What?

Mary★★★Kate: I'll fill U in later. Gotta jet!

AshleyO : Wait!

Mary★★★Kate is no longer available.

CHAPTER ELEVEN

It was a cool, breezy night. Mary-Kate gazed up at the moon as she and Trevor made their way down the beach.

It feels as if summer is already over, she thought wistfully as the salty wind grazed her skin. She tightened her shawl around her shoulders and shivered slightly. Autumn was definitely in the air. Or at least it was in her mind.

"Cold?" Trevor asked her.

"I'm okay," Mary-Kate replied.

They continued in silence down the deserted beach. They had gotten used to being silent with each other.

Ever since the Ferris wheel incident, it was as though they had an unspoken agreement not to talk about their relationship.

They still went on dates almost every night. In fact, their dates seemed more fun and romantic than ever.

But if they talked at all, they talked about work, their friends, movies, stuff like that. They never talked about what they *needed* to talk about, which was the inevitable: What would happen at the end of summer, when it was time for them to go their separate ways to college?

They also hadn't talked about the other thing: how they really felt about each other. Neither Trevor nor Mary-Kate had said the three big words, *I love you*, to each other.

Trevor wrapped an arm around Mary-Kate's shoulders and pointed to a big rock. "Wanna sit?"

"Sure." Mary-Kate smiled. It was a beautiful spot, with a view of the old lighthouse out on a jetty.

They sat down very close together on the rock. Trevor took her hand. "So," he said.

"So," Mary-Kate echoed.

She glanced at Trevor's profile. He looked nervous, as though he had something on his mind but didn't know how to say it.

"Go ahead, spit it out," Mary-Kate said lightly.

He turned to look at her. His brown eyes were troubled. "Mary-Kate," he began. "I want to . . . that is, we really should . . . that is, we really need to discuss . . ." His voice trailed off.

"College," Mary-Kate finished for him. She squeezed his hand. "It's okay. I know we kind of got into a major fight the last time we talked about it. But we really *do* need to discuss it."

Trevor looked relieved. "Yeah. The thing is, I really

hate it that you're going three thousand miles away," he blurted out.

"I know," Mary-Kate said. "I feel that way, too. It's, like, halfway around the planet. Well, not exactly, but it *feels* that way."

"I suppose we *could* do the long-distance thing," Trevor pointed out. "Other people do it."

"That's true," Mary-Kate agreed. She wondered what that would be like, only seeing each other every few months. Would it be exciting, like having to be apart at the stables? Or would it be awful and lonely?

"We'd run up some pretty major phone bills," Trevor added.

"I guess we'd only be able to see each other at Thanksgiving, Christmas, winter break, spring break, and then next summer," Mary-Kate calculated.

Trevor was silent for a long moment. Then he said, "Hey. Would you . . . I mean, do you think you might consider staying here and going to my school?" he asked her shyly.

"Oh!" Mary-Kate said. She didn't want to tell him that she'd been thinking the very same thing. Although she still hadn't finished the application for his school. The basics were easy, but the essay portion was holding her up. She'd have to do some fancy writing to convince the Pacific School of Design that she was really serious about graphic arts.

"Sure. Of course I'd consider it. Or maybe you

could consider going to *my* school," she added.

"Wouldn't it be easier for you to just stay here?" Trevor asked her.

"Why? It would be just as easy for both of us to go east," Mary-Kate replied.

Trevor shrugged. "I don't know. It makes more sense if we both stay here. That way, neither of us has to move all the way across the country."

"Hey, Lawton's a great school. It's worth moving all the way across the country for," Mary-Kate snapped.

"Okay, fine, if it's such a great school, go!" Trevor said irritably.

"Fine!"

"Fine!"

Mary-Kate's eyes stung with tears. She couldn't believe they were fighting again—just like on the Ferris wheel.

"I'm out of here," she said, jumping to her feet. "Don't bother walking me home. I know how to get there."

"Mary-Kate!"

Mary-Kate ignored him and started walking down the beach. But something—inside her heart—stopped her. Without thinking, without even knowing what she was doing, she stopped in her tracks, turned, and shouted, "I love you!"

Tears were flowing down her face now. Trevor leapt to his feet and ran to her. He wrapped her in his warm embrace and lifted her into the air. "I love you, too, Mary-Kate," he whispered happily. "I love you, too."

When her feet touched the ground, Mary-Kate realized that she was crying and laughing at the same time against Trevor's chest. He held her face in both his hands and kissed her lips, ever so gently, then more passionately.

And then they just held each other for a long time, huddling against the chilly August wind, listening to the waves crashing against the shore.

Mary***Kate invites Felicity_girl, Claude18, and AshleyO to Instant Message!

Mary***Kate: He said it!

AshleyO: Who said what?

Mary***Kate: I LOVE U.

AshleyO: I love U 2.

Claude18: I think she means Trev.

AshleyO: Oh! Yea!

Felicity_girl: Congratulations, MK!
    It took him long enuf!

AshleyO: Did U say it back?

Mary***Kate: Actually, I said it first.

Felicity_girl: Yes! That's our girl!

Claude18: We should celebrate. Tomorrow
    night?

AshleyO: I might be busy.

Felicity_girl: Too bad!

Claude18: Plans with Ms. Solar Power?

Mary***Kate: Who's Ms. Solar Power?

AshleyO: Whoops! Customer! Gotta go.
    Signing off!!

CHAPTER TWELVE

The phone rang on Wednesday night, just as Mary-Kate was turning on an old sci-fi movie on TV. She knew it wasn't Trevor, because he was out having pizza with some of his buds.

She thought about letting the answering machine take care of it. She was too tired and low-energy to have a conversation with anyone, even if it consisted of taking a message for someone else in the family. But at the last second she changed her mind.

She picked up the phone. "Hello?"

"Hello, is this Mary-Kate?"

The girl's voice was unfamiliar to her. "Yup, this is Mary-Kate."

"This is Madison Andrews," the girl said. "I'm calling from New York. I just got a postcard from Lawton College. They've assigned me to be your roommate!"

"Oh! That is so cool that you called," Mary-Kate said. She sat up, feeling unexpectedly happy about the call. "So your name is Madison? Are you named after the avenue?" she asked eagerly.

Madison laughed. "No. I'm named after some really distant relative. My mother's great-aunt's cousin or something."

Mary-Kate laughed, too. "It's a great name, wherever it comes from."

"So what's L.A. like, anyway? Do you go to the beach every day?" Madison asked.

Mary-Kate told her all about life in Los Angeles. Then Madison told Mary-Kate all about her life in New York City and that she had already been to visit the Lawton campus. Mary-Kate thought that it sounded amazing. So much to do! So many things to see! Her pulse raced just at the thought of it.

"I'll take you to my favorite cafés," Madison offered. "Oh, and I know the best place to get really cheap vintage clothes."

"That sounds awesome," Mary-Kate agreed.

"There's also a great Chinatown here, where we can get killer dorm room decor," Madison went on. "They have really pretty silk wall hangings and paper lanterns and stuff like that."

"Definitely," Mary-Kate said enthusiastically.

And then Mary-Kate remembered Trevor. They had not yet decided what to do about their college dilemma. Would he go east with her? Would she stay out west with him? Or would they simply go their separate ways and try to keep their relationship alive through e-mail, phone calls, and school vacations?

"Hey? You still there?" Madison asked her.

"I'm here. I was just thinking about my boyfriend. He lives in L.A.," Mary-Kate explained.

"Oh," Madison said sympathetically. "That's tough. It'll be hard to leave him, huh?"

"Uh . . . yeah." Suddenly Mary-Kate didn't want to talk about Trevor anymore. She didn't want to talk, period.

"Listen, let's stay in touch, okay? Give me your e-mail address, and I'll give you mine," Mary-Kate told Madison hastily.

The two of them exchanged their contact info, then said good-bye. Mary-Kate hung up, then clicked off the TV. She headed upstairs to her room.

She reached into her desk and pulled out the half-completed application for Trevor's college. Then she picked up a pen and began to write.

Ashley threw her keys and backpack onto the front hall table. It was almost midnight. She couldn't wait to crawl into bed.

It had been a long day at work, followed by burgers and shakes with Kim at a restaurant she liked called the Disheveled Dog. Kim had been a really good friend, letting Ashley vent about Felicity and Claudia and how much they'd changed. Toward the end of the evening Kim had even offered to go out for manicures to cheer Ashley up.

"But I thought manicures were against your principles, or whatever," Ashley had pointed out.

"Hey, you gotta compromise once in a while. After all, what are friends for?" Kim had replied.

Ashley had taken a rain check on the manicures, since it was so late. They had agreed to do it on Friday night, after their last day at work.

And now Ashley was ready for bed.

But when she got upstairs, she noticed that Mary-Kate's light was still on. She knocked lightly on her sister's door. "Mary-Kate?" she whispered. "It's me."

A second later Mary-Kate opened the door. She was still dressed. "Hey."

"You're still up?" Ashley asked her, curious.

Mary-Kate nodded. "Come on in. It feels like I haven't seen you in forever."

"I know," Ashley agreed.

"We still have to finalize our Joshua Tree trip," Mary-Kate reminded her. "By the way, Mom and Dad said okay, as long as we bring our cells and Mom's pager and register our exact location with the park ranger and call them twice a day and—"

"I think the trip is off," Ashley announced.

Mary-Kate gasped. *"What?"*

Ashley hadn't even admitted it to herself until just that minute. But there was no way she could go through with this camping trip—not with the way Felicity and Claudia had been acting. How could they celebrate the end of a summer that had never really jelled for the four of them?

"We *have* to go," Mary-Kate insisted. "The four of us planned this together, remember?"

"Yeah, well, *two* of us have totally forgotten about it," Ashley replied dryly.

Mary-Kate frowned. "You mean Felicity and Claudia?"

Ashley nodded. "When we reminded them about it when they were in Spain, they totally spaced out. It was like, 'Joshua *who*?'"

"Look, they were probably distracted by Ashton Kutcher, or whatever," Mary-Kate rationalized.

"And then when they came back, they were putting down camping because it wouldn't be in a four-star hotel," Ashley went on.

Mary-Kate sighed. "Okay, so their brains are still in Spain. But I know they want to go. Felicity called me today and wanted to know if the trip was still on. She said she left you two messages to call her, but you hadn't returned them. She thought the trip was off."

"Well, she's right. The trip *is* off," Ashley snapped.

Mary-Kate sat down on her bed and patted the spot next to her. "Sit. Tell me what's going on," she said sympathetically.

Ashley sat down and proceeded to tell her about the way Felicity and Claudia had been acting ever since they came back from Spain.

"They're in their own little universe," Ashley finished. "I don't think they really want to go to Joshua Tree. I think Felicity was just saying that to be polite, or something."

Mary-Kate looked troubled. "But we *have* to go," she said, her voice trembling. "It's more important than ever!"

Ashley was taken aback. Her sister looked really upset suddenly. "Why?"

"Because," Mary-Kate replied. Her glanced drifted over to her computer monitor. Ashley saw a photograph of some books and a diploma on the screen.

"Mary-Kate, what's up?" Ashley asked her quietly.

Mary-Kate took a deep breath. "I've been thinking. I'm not sure I want to go east this fall. I've been . . . I've been seriously considering staying in L.A. with Trevor. In fact, I just sent in an application to his college."

Ashley stared at Mary-Kate, trying to make sense of what she had just said. "No," she said finally. "You're joking, right?"

Mary-Kate smiled sadly and shook her head. "No, I'm *not* joking."

Ashley was too stunned to speak. This couldn't be happening. She knew Mary-Kate and Trevor were in love. But this was college! How could Mary-Kate give up her first-choice school for a guy?

"Look," Ashley said finally, trying to keep her voice

level. "I know you and Trevor love each other. And I know you don't want to be separated from him. But how can you change your major life plans for him— just like *that*?"

"This college was always your idea," Mary-Kate blurted out.

"What?" Ashley cried out.

Mary-Kate glanced at her feet. "I didn't want to hurt your feelings. But it was kind of your idea for us to go to Lawton together. I'm not sure that it's as important to me as it is to you."

Ashley just sat there. Her whole body felt numb, in shock. She didn't know what to say.

"I'm sorry, Ash," Mary-Kate whispered.

Ashley shook her head. "No, it's okay. Well, maybe it's not okay."

"I'm sorry," Mary-Kate repeated.

Ashley's thoughts were racing. Her perfect summer had been going downhill from the beginning: no law firm job, no Felicity and Claudia, and too little time with Mary-Kate. Now it had totally crashed and burned.

This was beyond anything she'd ever imagined. It was one thing to have a not-so-perfect three months. But four years without Mary-Kate? That was unthinkable.

Mary-Kate leaned over and gave Ashley a hug. "I haven't made up my mind yet," she reminded her.

"I know," Ashley replied glumly. "I just hope you won't decide until we get back from Joshua Tree. You really need to give this some serious thought."

Mary-Kate grinned at Ashley. "Does this mean we're going to Joshua Tree, after all?"

Ashley nodded. No way was she going to miss spending this precious time with her sister. "Definitely!" she replied.

AshleyO invites Felicity_girl, Claude18, and Mary***Kate to Instant Message!

AshleyO: So who's up for Joshua Tree on
    Saturday?

Claude18: Me!

Felicity_girl: Me! But I kinda got the
    vibe that U didn't want 2 go, Ash.

AshleyO: Sorry. I'll explain everything
    Sat. Will U come?

Felicity_girl: Totally. I've already
    packed the freeze-dried nachos.

AshleyO: Gross me out!

Mary***Kate: Who's driving?

AshleyO: We're driving. See U all brite
    and early Sat morning!

Claude18: Who's bringing the breakfast
    smoothies?

CHAPTER THIRTEEN

This is the best," Ashley said.

"Yeah, definitely," Mary-Kate agreed.

Ashley gazed up at the sky and sighed happily. The desert sky was nothing like the city sky. Far from the bright lights of the city, every star, every constellation seemed to be visible.

Felicity leaned toward the blazing campfire to toast a marshmallow. "Did any of you notice? It's totally quiet here," she said in a low voice.

Claudia nodded. "No cars. No music. No wild parties."

"Just a bunch of campers, the park ranger, and some cacti," Ashley said. She picked up her stick and took a bite of her marshmallow. It was golden brown and gooey and totally yummy.

Just then there was a low beeping sound. Ashley realized it was her cell. "That's me," she announced.

"I guess it's not so quiet here after all," Claudia joked.

Ashley pulled her cell out of her jacket pocket.

Someone was sending her an Instant Message. The screen read: U GIRLS OK? LOVE, DAD.

Ashley smiled. "It's our dad," she explained to the others. She punched in a reply: A-OK. LOVE, A.

"Do they *have* to IM us twelve times a day?" Felicity giggled.

"Hey, they love us. I guess." Mary–Kate grinned.

Claudia turned to Ashley. "I'm really glad this trip happened after all."

Ashley nodded. "Yeah, me, too."

Ashley realized that Felicity and Claudia were looking at her. She knew they were waiting for an explanation—an explanation as to why the trip had almost *not* happened.

"Listen," Ashley said slowly. "I know things have been kind of weird between us since you guys got back from Spain."

"*Weird*, as in you wouldn't return our calls?" Felicity said gently.

Ashley smiled apologetically. "Yeah. See, it's just that, ever since the Spain thing, you guys seem so . . . different. You have this superclose bond now. And I kind of . . . well, I kind of feel left out," she blurted out.

"Oh, Ash!" Claudia cried out. "That's awful. I'm so sorry!"

"Yeah," Felicity agreed. "We've been so wrapped up in our Spain trip, I'm sure it's been totally obnoxious. We're so sorry!"

Ashley grinned. She felt so much better, now that she had told her friends the truth. "That's okay. I'm just glad you're back."

"We didn't know why you'd been ignoring us ever since we got back. We thought that maybe you'd replaced us with a new best friend. That girl Kim," Claudia said.

Ashley shook her head. "Kim is a good friend. But she could never replace you guys," she said, meaning it.

Ashley got up and hugged both Felicity and Claudia. Then she turned to Mary-Kate. "Okay, now that I've spilled my guts, you spill *your* guts."

Mary-Kate frowned. "What are you talking about?"

"You know," Ashley reminded her.

Mary-Kate blushed. "Oh, yeah. Well. Okay, so I'm thinking of staying in L.A. with Trevor instead of going east with Ashley," she announced to Felicity and Claudia.

"What?" they cried out in unison.

"Are you crazy, girl?" Felicity demanded. "I can't believe you're thinking of staying in California. For a *guy!*"

"What about meeting *new* guys?" Claudia asked her.

"Don't you want to have new adventures?" Felicity added.

"And what about all your dreams and aspirations and stuff like that?" Claudia asked.

"Not to mention the excellent shopping in New York City?" Felicity reminded her.

Mary-Kate kept nodding. "I know, I know!" she wailed. "I'm really torn. I don't know what to do!"

"It's your decision," Ashley said. "And we'll stand by you no matter what you decide. Right, Fel? Right, Claudia?"

Felicity and Claudia exchanged a glance.

"Definitely," Felicity said.

"That's what friends are for," Claudia added. "Our lives may be totally changing, but *we're* going to stay rock-solid, no matter what happens." She smiled and swiped at her eyes. "Hey, that was kind of deep. I'm tearing up. Ash, pass the marshmallows."

The four girls put fresh marshmallows onto their sticks and dipped them into the fire. As Ashley watched her marshmallow sizzle, she thought of a brilliant idea.

"Hey," she said. "I just thought of something. Let's make this camping trip an annual tradition. That way, no matter what happens in the future, we'll always have this to look forward to."

"I love it!" Mary-Kate said enthusiastically.

"I'm down with that," Felicity agreed. Claudia nodded.

They smiled at one another and raised their marshmallow sticks in the air.

"To us," Ashley said.

"To us!" Mary-Kate, Felicity, and Claudia echoed.

• • •

The cold desert air brushed Mary-Kate's cheeks, waking her up. She blinked into the sunlight. It was morning. She had no idea what time it was, though.

She glanced around the tent and saw Ashley buried in her sleeping bag, snoring softly. As quietly as possible Mary-Kate got up, slipped on a sweater, and headed outside.

Felicity and Claudia seemed to be asleep in their tent, too. The sun was just starting to come up, and the sky was aflame with streaks of gold and pink and amber. Mary-Kate walked to the campfire and sat down next to it. A few smoldering embers glowed in the ashes. In the distance, a bird rustled through the brush.

Mary-Kate stared at the embers and folded her arms over her chest to keep warm. She had been up most of the night, thinking.

She kept going over the conversation she'd had with Trevor two nights ago.

"What would you think if I stayed in L.A. and went to your school?"

"Really? You'd do that?"

"I'm seriously thinking about it."

"I just don't want you to resent me later though. Like you gave up your dream school just to be with me."

"I'll make my final decision at Joshua Tree, okay?"

Mary-Kate looked up at the sky. The colors were

even more vivid now. She thought she had never seen anything so . . . beautiful. There was no other word for it. Mary-Kate had had no idea that such a beautiful place existed in the world.

And she never would have found out if she hadn't come on this camping adventure with Ashley and their friends.

Then she glanced down at her silver charm bracelet with its single dangling heart. She hadn't taken it off all summer.

Mary-Kate nodded. She had made her decision. She knew what she had to do.

AshleyO invites Felicity_girl, Claude18, and Mary★★★Kate to Instant Message!

AshleyO: Did everyone survive post-
   camping-trip parental interrogation?

Claude18: Yeah.

Felicity_girl: Anyone else find sand in
   their underwear?

AshleyO: Or dead bugs?

Felicity-girl: MK, did U make your
   decision yet?

Mary★★★Kate: I've gotta go talk 2
   Trevor.

AshleyO: Mary-Kate!

Mary★★★Kate: I'll talk 2 you all later.
   Signing off.

CHAPTER FOURTEEN

Mary-Kate knocked on Trevor's door. She glanced at her watch: 7:00 P.M. He had told her on the phone that he would be around all evening.

The door opened. Mary-Kate's heart skipped a beat, as it always did, when she saw Trevor's supercute face. He looked even cuter than usual because his brown hair was tousled, as though he'd just gotten up from a nap.

"Hey," Mary-Kate said, smiling.

"Hey," Trevor said softly. He held out his arms. She nestled into his chest, inhaling his familiar fragrance, loving the warmth of him. Even though they had only been apart for three days, it felt more like three weeks.

They sat down on the steps of his front porch. He hooked an arm around her shoulders and kissed her neck. "I missed you," he said.

"I missed you, too," Mary-Kate replied.

"How was Joshua Tree?"

"Great. Listen . . ."

"You made your decision," Trevor said, understanding. His voice trembled every so slightly.

Mary-Kate nodded. "I've decided to go to Lawton after all."

Trevor was silent. "Okay," he said after a moment.

"I hope you're not mad at me," Mary-Kate pleaded. "It's just that I had a lot of time to think while I was in the desert. And I realized a lot of things. I really, really love California. But I need to experience new places. And I'll never see those new places if I don't go looking."

Trevor nodded. "Yeah. I totally understand."

"You do?" Mary-Kate asked eagerly.

"I do," Trevor replied, smiling. "I'm bummed, but I totally understand."

"I know we can't make any rules about what's going to happen in our future," Mary-Kate went on. "We should just do what feels right and take it as it comes."

"Yeah, I agree."

Mary-Kate gazed into Trevor's eyes. When he kissed her, his kiss told her everything she needed to know: *He loves me!*

It was the biggest bonfire Ashley had ever seen. There were dozens of kids dancing around it, swinging their arms in the air. The boom box was blasting one of her favorite No Doubt songs. In the background a banner swayed in the breeze: GOOD–BYE SUMMER! HERE WE COME, COLLEGE!

It was the last beach party of the summer. Soon everyone would be packing up and going away to school.

Ashley took a sip of her cherry soda and glanced around. Practically everyone from Ocean View High was at the party. And Mary-Kate had invited a bunch of friends from the riding stables including a girl named Aisha and her new boyfriend, Grant.

Even Kim had come to the party at Ashley's invitation. In fact, Kim was hanging out at the food table with Felicity and Claudia. The three of them were chowing down on pizza and laughing about something.

Ashley couldn't believe it. Her three friends were getting along!

"Hey, Ash."

Ashley turned around. Mary-Kate was standing there, a big smile on her face.

"Hey, Miss East Coast College!" Ashley called out.

"Hey, Miss East Coast College, yourself," Mary-Kate replied.

Mary-Kate had told her the good news—the *great* news—a few nights ago, right after she told Trevor. Ashley was so happy that Mary-Kate would be going east after all. She hadn't wanted to say anything to Mary-Kate but the thought of going three thousand miles away without her had been totally and absolutely terrifying for Ashley.

"You having fun?" Mary-Kate asked her.

"Uh-huh. I think this is the best beach party we've ever had," Ashley replied.

"I'm going to miss everyone," Mary-Kate said, looking around wistfully.

"I know. Me, too," Ashley said. "You know, I've been thinking . . ."

"Sounds dangerous," Mary-Kate joked.

Ashley chuckled. "I've been thinking. I was going to major in pre-law in college. But now I'm not so sure. I've been thinking I might take some psych courses. I mean, the human mind seems *way* more interesting than legal technicalities."

"My sister, Ms. Freud," Mary-Kate teased her.

"Ha-ha," Ashley said. "I don't know about that. It's just that I don't want to miss out on any cool opportunities because of a bunch of preconceived ideas I have about my future, such as, I must be a lawyer. I want to go into the future with an open mind."

"Wow, sounds deep," Mary-Kate said. "And really brave!"

"It's the new me," Ashley said with a grin. "Besides, it's easy to be brave now that I know you'll be coming east with me."

Mary-Kate smiled and gave her a hug. Ashley hugged her, too.

Just then Ashley's cell phone rang. "Sorry," Ashley said, extricating herself. She clicked on the phone. "Hello?"

"Hey, Ashley? It's Zoe."

Oh, no. Zoe! Ashley had been meaning to call her future roommate. She really, really needed to put her foot down about Zoe's proposed all-leopard décor for their room, the all-night clubbing, and everything else. Kim had encouraged her to 'fess up and give Zoe a chance before changing roommates. So had Mary-Kate, Felicity, and Claudia. But somehow Ashley hadn't been able to bring herself to do it.

But it was now or never. "Listen, Zoe," Ashley said. Mary-Kate looked at her and raised her eyebrows. "I've been meaning to call you and talk to you about something."

"Oh?"

"You know how you wanted to decorate our room all-leopard?" Ashley reminded her. "The truth is . . . I kind of, um, hate that idea."

Much to Ashley's surprise, Zoe burst into laughter. "Really? What a relief! Me, too," she confessed. "I just said that because, you know, I didn't want you to think I was a total hick. I wanted you to think I was cool and sophisticated."

"Omigosh," Ashley said. "You don't need to impress me! You seem great just the way you are." She added, "So what kind of decor *do* you want?"

"Actually, I kind of want some nice floral bed-spreads and some pink throw pillows."

Ashley gave Mary-Kate the thumbs-up sign. "Me, too," she told Zoe. "That sounds perfect!"

"Really?"

"Really." Ashley laughed. "Hey, and the all-night clubbing?"

"I fall asleep at nine," Zoe confessed.

Ashley giggled. "I have a feeling we're going to be great friends."

"I'm going to call you every day."

"Me, too. And don't forget the three-hour time difference."

"New York is three hours ahead, right?"

"Right. I'll be done with my first class before you're even awake!"

Trevor laughed. Mary-Kate laughed, too, and leaned into his shoulder.

The two of them were sitting on the beach, away from the rest of the party. They had both taken off their shoes and were waiting for the waves to reach their bare feet.

"Don't forget about e-mail and IMs," Mary-Kate reminded him.

"Don't worry. I won't forget. I'm going to be writing you and bugging you all day long," Trevor joked.

"Sounds great," Mary-Kate said, meaning it.

"Do you want to come home for Thanksgiving, or do you want me to visit you out there?" Trevor asked her.

"Let's talk to our parents about it. Either way sounds totally fine. And I'll definitely come home for Christmas," Mary-Kate told him.

A wave washed up the shore and over their feet. Mary-Kate laughed and shivered at the sensation of cold water against her bare skin.

At the same time it felt like a sign. A *good* sign. *Everything was going to be okay,* Mary-Kate thought.

"Hey, I almost forgot something," Trevor said. "I have a surprise for you."

"You do?" Mary-Kate asked him, curious. "What?"

Trevor reached into his pocket and pulled out her silver charm bracelet. He had borrowed it back from her a few days ago.

"I had it engraved, just like I promised," Trevor told her softly.

Mary-Kate took the bracelet from him. Her heart was racing as she held the charm up to the moonlight.

The charm had been engraved in small, old-fashioned-looking script. It read: LOVE ALWAYS, TREVOR.

"Oh." Mary-Kate sighed. "It's perfect."

Trevor kissed the tip of her nose. "I love you, Mary-Kate."

"I love you, Trevor."

Trevor fastened the bracelet on her wrist, then held her tightly. As Mary-Kate nestled in his arms, she thought that no matter what happened now or in the future, everything—*everything*—was going to be just fine.

Book 3
Everything I Want

"Whatever you do, do *not* panic," Ashley advised.

Mary-Kate gazed around in dismay. "Does that include yelling for help?"

Two airplane and one shuttle rides later, the sisters were at long last standing on their new college campus, in front of what was supposed to be their dorm. Despite the fading daylight, it looked as lovely as it had in the catalogue. Originally a mansion from the Victorian era, it was a tall and stately brick building with sparkling leaded windows and a big brass knocker adorning the front door.

Unfortunately, the knocker wasn't the only thing the door was wearing. Ribbons of yellow hazard tape zigzagged across it, giving it the appearance of a crime scene. An enormous sign lettered in bold, black letters declared:

HAZARDOUS AREA. DO NOT ENTER UNDER ANY CIRCUMSTANCES.

"How about whining?" Mary-Kate asked now. "I know it's off-limits as a rule, but, where are we supposed to go? What are we supposed to do?"

"Olsen," a female voice suddenly announced.

Ashley turned to see a tall young woman with dark brown hair striding toward them purposefully, a clipboard clutched like a shield to her chest. She was dressed in a pair of faded blue jeans and a crisply pressed oxford cloth shirt.

"Are you the Olsen sisters, Mary-Kate and Ashley?" she asked.

"I'm Ashley, and this is Mary-Kate," Ashley said, as she extended her hand. The young woman took it, her grip brisk and firm.

"I'm Sharon Newton, your RA," she said. "Or, I will be your RA, just as soon as we get this mess under control."

"What happened?" Mary-Kate inquired.

"Water damage," Sharon Newton said. "A water main burst just yesterday. There are problems all over this part of town. We're hoping the damage to the dorm isn't too extensive, but, naturally making sure the building is safe for students is our first priority. Until that's done . . ." Her voice trailed off.

"But what happens to us in the meantime?" Mary-Kate inquired. "All of us who are supposed to live here, I mean. How many does this dorm hold?"

"About twenty-five," Sharon answered. "Most are double rooms, but there are a couple of singles and a three-person suite. We're finding accommodations where we can, trying to keep students as close to campus as possible. You guys actually have it pretty good." She pivoted on one heel and pointed to a set of townhouses directly across the street. "You'll be right over there. The townhouse with the mums in the windowboxes."

"That's fantastic!" Ashley declared.

Though not as old as the building which would, eventually, be their dorm, the townhouses were also made of brick and very definitely charming.

"There are a couple of things that you should know about the place before I give you your keys," Sharon Newton said. "First and foremost, the house belongs to one of our professors who's away this semester on sabbatical."

"A professor's house!" Mary-Kate exclaimed. "Bet that doesn't happen very often."

"You'd be right," Sharon acknowledged. "You were chosen because your records, Ashley's in particular, demonstrate a high degree of reliability."

"In other words, rule number one is *Don't Trash the Professor's Place*," Mary-Kate commented.

"Also rules two through ten," Sharon said with a smile. "Never forget you're in the home of a professor, particularly considering you may end up in one of his classes down the road!"

"Yikes! Okay, we'll remember," Mary-Kate promised.

Sharon consulted her clipboard for a moment. "I see by my notes that your roommates, Zoe Hanover and Madison Andrews, have already moved in. Hope you like the rooms they chose. Let me give you your keys, and you'll be all set." She produced an envelope with OLSEN written in crisp, precise handwriting across the top. She opened it and tipped two keys out into her palm.

"Here you go," she said. "The one key opens both the front door lock and the deadbolt. Any questions?"

"How can we contact you if we need you?" Ashley inquired.

At this, Sharon Newton reached into her jacket pocket and extracted two small, white business cards.

"I had this made up for all my freshmen. It has my cell number and e-mail address," she said. "I'll do my best to see how you guys are settling in, but things may be pretty hectic for these first few days. I've got a lot of students to get straightened away between now and when school starts."

"Don't worry about us," Mary-Kate said quickly. "I'm sure we'll be just fine."

"If you have any questions or concerns, don't hesitate to be in touch," Sharon said. "I guess that's it, unless you want some help with those bags."

She eyed the pile of luggage with a look that Ashley could only describe as *doubtful*. She was just pulling in a breath to accept Sharon's offer when Mary-Kate spoke up.

"Oh, that's all right," she said breezily. "We got them this far, I'm sure we can get them across the street. It's only a little farther."

"If you say so," Sharon said, just as her cell phone began to warble. "Nice to have met you both. I'm sure I'll see you around."

With that, she strode off down the street at the same brisk pace with which she'd approached, cell phone pressed to one ear, speaking animatedly.

Mary-Kate picked up what Ashley couldn't help but notice were the lightest two of her suitcases.

"What are you waiting for?" she asked. "Come on. Let's go check things out!"

With that, she hurried across the street as fast as the big suitcases would allow.

Win the Best Party Ever!

You receive:

- Karaoke machine
- Fragrance
- Purses
- Cosmetics
- Hair Accessories
- CDs
- Videos

ONE LUCKY WINNER

gets to throw a great party for ten friends!

PLUS A $250 GIFT CHECK FOR PARTY FOOD AND GOODIES!

Mary-Kate and Ashley *Graduation Summer*
Best Party Ever Sweepstakes
OFFICIAL RULES:

1. NO PURCHASE OR PAYMENT NECESSARY TO ENTER OR WIN.

2. How to Enter. To enter, complete the official entry form or hand print your name, address, age and phone number along with the words "Graduation Summer Best Party Ever Sweepstakes" on a 3" x 5" card and mail to: Graduation Summer Best Party Ever Sweepstakes, c/o HarperEntertainment, Attn: Children's Marketing Department, 10 East 53rd Street, New York, NY 10022. Entries must be received no later than November 30, 2004. Enter as often as you wish, but each entry must be mailed separately. One entry per envelope. Partially completed, illegible, or mechanically reproduced entries will not be accepted. Sponsor is not responsible for lost, late, mutilated, illegible, stolen, postage due, incomplete, or misdirected entries. All entries become the property of Dualstar Entertainment Group, LLC, and will not be returned.

3. Eligibility. Sweepstakes open to all legal residents of the United States (excluding Colorado and Rhode Island) who are between the ages of five and fifteen on November 30, 2004 excluding employees and immediate family members of HarperCollins Publishers, Inc., ("HarperCollins"), Parachute Properties and Parachute Press, Inc., and their respective subsidiaries and affiliates, officers, directors, shareholders, employees, agents, attorneys, and other representatives and their immediate families (individually and collectively, "Parachute"), Dualstar Entertainment Group, LLC, and its subsidiaries and affiliates, officers, directors, shareholders, employees, agents, attorneys, and other representatives and their immediate families (individually and collectively, "Dualstar"), and their respective parent companies, affiliates, subsidiaries, advertising, promotion and fulfillment agencies, and the persons with whom each of the above are domiciled. All applicable federal, state and local laws and regulations apply. Offer void where prohibited or restricted by law.

4. Odds of Winning. Odds of winning depend on the total number of entries received. Approximately 300,000 sweepstakes announcements published. All prizes will be awarded. Winner will be randomly drawn on or about December 15, 2004 by HarperCollins, whose decision is final. Potential winner will be notified by mail and will be required to sign and return an affidavit of eligibility and release of liability within 14 days of notification. Prizes won by minors will be awarded to parent or legal guardian who must sign and return all required legal documents. By acceptance of their prize, winner consents to the use of their name, photograph, likeness, and biographical information by HarperCollins, Parachute, Dualstar, and for publicity purposes without further compensation except where prohibited.

5. Grand Prize. One Grand Prize Winner will win one karaoke machine, 10 Mary-Kate and Ashley back-to-school purses containing Mary-Kate and Ashley merchandise (party music CDs, videos, fragrance, cosmetics, hair accessories) and $250 to be used by winner toward the purchase of party goods and food. Approximate combined retail value of prize totals $1000.00.

6. Prize Limitations. All prizes will be awarded. Only one prize will be awarded per individual, family, or household. Prizes are non-transferable and cannot be sold or redeemed for cash. No cash substitute is available. Any federal, state, or local taxes are the responsibility of the winner. Sponsor may substitute prize of equal or greater value, if necessary, due to availability.

7. Additional terms: By participating, entrants agree a) to the official rules and decisions of the judges, which will be final in all respects; and to waive any claim to ambiguity of the official rules and b) to release, discharge, and hold harmless HarperCollins, Warner, Parachute, Dualstar, and their respective parent companies, affiliates, subsidiaries, employees and representatives and advertising, promotion and fulfillment agencies from and against any and all liability or damages associated with acceptance, use, or misuse of any prize received or participation in any Sweepstakes-related activity or participation in this Sweepstakes.

8. Dispute Resolution. Any dispute arising from this Sweepstakes will be determined according to the laws of the State of New York, without reference to its conflict of law principles, and the entrants consent to the personal jurisdiction of the State and Federal courts located in New York County and agree that such courts have exclusive jurisdiction over all such disputes.

9. Winner Information. To obtain the name of the winner, please send your request and a self-addressed stamped envelope (residents of Vermont may omit return postage) to Graduation Summer Best Party Ever Winner, c/o HarperEntertainment, 10 East 53rd Street, New York, NY 10022 by April 1, 2005.

10. Sweepstakes Sponsor: HarperCollins Publishers, Inc.

Mary-Kate and Ashley's

GRADUATION SUMMER

is about to begin!

Senior prom, graduation, saying good-bye to old friends and making new ones. For Mary-Kate and Ashley, this is the summer that will change their lives forever . . . *Graduation Summer*. And they can't wait!

NEW

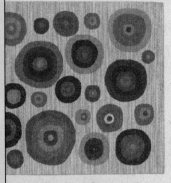

Travel the world with **Mary-Kate** and **Ashley**
www.mary-kateandashley.com

Mary-Kate Olsen   Ashley Olsen

the movie

Experience the same hilarious trials and tribulations as Roxy and Jane did in their feature film *New York Minute*.

Bonus Movie Mini-Poster!